Spirits of Suburbia

Ordinary people, Extraordinary Tales

Edited by

Elizabeth Hirst and Jennifer Bickley

To David,
A cornucopia of stories,
just for you! Enjoy!
Much Love,
Elizabeth Hirst

Thanks so much David!
May your life's staircase always lead up!
Jennifer Bickley

Other Printed Works by Pop Seagull Publishing

Novels

Flood Waters Rising
Distant Early Warning (Coming Spring 2014)

Anthologies

Monsters and Mist

Visit Pop Seagull Publishing on the Web, at:

http://popseagullpublishing.wordpress.com

Copyright 2013 by Pop Seagull Publishing
All rights reserved. No part of this book may be used or reproduced in any manner whatsoever without the written permission of Pop Seagull Publishing. For reprint permissions, please contact Elizabeth Hirst at lizmclean.artist@gmail.com

All characters in this book are fictitious. Any resemblance to persons living or dead is strictly coincidental.

Cover Design Copyright 2013 by Elizabeth Hirst
Published by
Pop Seagull Publishing
Oakville, Ontario, Canada

Printed and bound in the USA

Table of Contents

Acknowledgements	5
Seedlings	7
To Zombie Or Not To Zombie	13
Ghosts In My Hair	37
Dakota Is A Dryad's Name	45
The Staircase Leading Up	47
No Good Deed Goes Unpunished	63
The Home Tree	73
About The Authors	83
Bonus Material	87

Acknowledgements

First of all, I would like to thank all of the readers who bought our books, kept up with us, and came by to offer kind words of encouragement during our appearances and online. Pop Seagull is about you, first and foremost, and I couldn't be happier with the positive response we've recieved in our first two years of business. Without your support, this little volume would not exist.

Secondly, I would like to thank everyone who submitted stories for the anthology, and everyone who listened to my pitch for it with patience. I hope I've done right by you, and treated you as I would like to be treated. You have truly made my first foray into publishing others a delight.

And last, but certainly not least, I would like to thank our contibutors. Ira, thank you for your humor and your willingess to go above and beyond to see a quality product on the shelves. Jenn, thank you for your tireless work and encouragement on my behalf, and I hope that someday I can thank you even half as well as you deserve. Tecuma, thank you for burning that midnight oil, and for taking a chance on me.

With love and gratitude,

Elizabeth Hirst, Editor and President, Pop Seagull Publishing

Spirits of Suburbia

Seedlings
Elizabeth Hirst

Zinnia walked out of the salon on Sunday feeling like a million bucks. It took a half hour on Monday and a single sentence out of Jordan's mouth to send her back to being a bent penny forgotten on the railroad tracks.

Zinnia replayed it over and over in her mind, all during math. He swung by her like a train on the way to somewhere, looked her up and down and said, "Hey Zinnia, what's with your arms? Maybe you should get that checked out."

Apparently, she could make her hair as bright as a road flare (ombre dye job with sunset orange on top and fire-engine red working out to the ends) and still all people would notice was the eczema. Or the psoriasis. Or whatever the doctor-of-the-week claimed the little pink flakes flying off her skin for the last three months were a symptom of. As she wallowed in misery, she picked at some of the flakes without even thinking of it.

She realized too late that several large flakes had dislodged from her arm and floated ever so slowly toward the floor. Mandy Cho looked down at the flakes, then up at Zinnia, disgust and shock playing across her features. Why, oh why did they have to sit at these big group desks?

Mandy shifted her chair over loudly enough to make a couple of neighbours look too.

Eww, she mouthed silently, shaking her head as if Zinnia should have known better. Hadn't any of these people ever had chicken pox and had to wear those stupid mitts? Most of the time, she could control where her hands went, but when she got concentrating on something, it was like a reflex. They just started scratching of their own accord. And math...well, she wasn't the worst in it, but she did need to keep her mind on the equations and not the itch.

During break, she rushed to the bathroom and pulled out a medicine vial full of Useless Cream #6 (TM). She slathered it on her arms and neck in front of the mirror, gritting her teeth as she did. No matter how much she washed, the flakes kept coming, washing around in the cream, making it feel gross and gritty on her skin and drying up in long pink tidal marks when the cream absorbed in. She knew she looked a mess, but it was June, for Christ's sake. She couldn't just wear a sweater at this time of year.

After ten minutes, her skin felt just as dry and itchy as the last time. With one sad look back at herself in the mirror, she left the bathroom a stripy pathetic mess. She liked herself, generally... she had pretty, green, almond-shaped eyes and a delicate, pointy-chinned face with high cheekbones, that made her Mom speculate often that her birth mother must have been Russian or Ukrainian. Whatever she was, she had given Zinnia a dancer's figure. But as she walked down the hall, drowning in her Dad's t-shirt and jeans (she'd ruined all her own) people just stared at her arms and neck and hands, some avoiding eye contact, many giggling behind their hands or whispering.

Just one more week to summer, and then she could quietly flake away in peace.

Zinnia closed her eyes, and the shadows of the leaves above her felt like they were caressing her face and eyelids with an interplay of light and dark. Just light, and wind, and the Home Tree for three whole months.

At three, when the Monctons had first adopted her, the thing she remembered most clearly was the giant, gnarled maple outlined against the sky. Back then, the land behind their house was a stretch of fallow fields, and the tree grew there as if just for her, glorious, dark arms stretched out in welcome and flipping leaves waving hello. Over time, she had felt like she, too had put down roots in the black, moist soil, and any talk of moving away from this symbol of home, the Home Tree, would have broken her heart.

Today she lay, eyes closed, with her back slumped against the base of the trunk. She felt the bark, caressing the cracks and crevices, and her hand came away damp and covered in the fine, sooty dust that maples cover everything within fifty feet of them with between June and October.

"You're flaky too, but nobody seems to mind," she said absently, "Symbol of our country is a flake like me."

Mom called out the back door.

"Zinny, we're going now."

Zinnia rolled her eyes. They had said they were going at breakfast. They were just still hoping she'd opt for humiliation at the beach over a quiet solo picnic at home. She could just see it now... Everybody off of the beach! Pollution levels are way too high...Oh wait, that's just Zinnia leaving a trail of skin behind her. Somebody get the pool skimmer!

"Have fun, you guys," she called, "I'll leave my cell on."

The screen door slammed and then, just the cicadas, and far away, the sound of a truck backing up at the new warehouse beyond their property line. The air developed that sleepy, cuddling closeness that characterizes all the best summer days, and soon, Zinnia felt like a nap might be in order before lunch.

In the darkness before she opened her eyelids, Zinnia felt nothing but the crawling itch on her skin and the grass at her back...until she realized that her skin was moving, no insects were moving, all over her, everywhere.

She spat and shook and slapped at herself as she sat up, sending a multitude of ants flying into the grass in all directions. Big ones, little ones, red ones, black ones, the kind with wings...six anthills must have emptied just to walk on her. She stood up, still slapping at herself and crying out in disgust.

"What the hell? This is what I get for using Mom's cheap sunscreen!"

When they were all off, and she had looked through every fold of her clothing for stowaways, she leaned against the Home Tree.

"How do you do it?" she said to it, heaving a great sigh. Then, with her arm up to her face, she noticed: no flakes. The itch was gone too! Her mind felt blissfully clear, free of the nagging drone of constant discomfort.

A wind blew up, and through a drift of falling maple keys, she saw the ants carrying her skin, in flakes large and small, all in a line heading next door, over the wooden fence. What in the world...

She ran to the fence, jumping over the ants as she went, and then peered over the top. The line stretched out over the Divinskis' lawn, then through the chain links to the Gardeners' until they stretched out of sight over another wooden fence like her own. There were so many of them that they looked like a moving lichen spot.

She got down from the fence and ran to the short chain link divider that ran along the back of the warehouse lot. She hopped the fence, barely even pausing when the fence caught on Dad's huge shirt and scratched her side. She ran down the rows of houses, following the ants further down the street than she had ever gone on her bike, toward the stand of forest that belonged to the provincial park.

At the end of the line of ants stood a girl, thin like Zinnia, with the same grace of features, and about the same age, but with skin as dark as unsweetened coffee. Her hair, close-cropped, wrapped her head in an inch of jet black curls. The ants twined around her arms and legs, swirling like the center of a storm.

She smiled, and Zinnia, despite being more than a little frightened, had to smile too. She looked so beautiful, so remarkable standing there, in the sunlight, in a plain orange tank top and jean shorts, and Zinnia knew that it had nothing to do with the ants.

"I was hoping you'd come," the girl said, "I wanted to meet you."

Zinnia stood there for a moment, not knowing what to do. Her heart pounded, and this all had a profound feeling of wrongness, like when you wake up from a dream that's just one twist of reality away from your life. And yet, that feeling in her gut, the one that told her when to stay and when to go, when to sleep, and eat, and what her favourite things were...that part felt right, in a way that it seldom ever had. In fact, the last time she had felt this... right...was in the fleeting, blurry memories that she had of her birth mother, looking up at her face into blue sky and tree branches, not caring that her hair was gone, or her cheeks were hollow, but rather that she was there, and the day was there, and the tree was there, shading them both.

The girl gestured to a gate in the back fence. Zinnia had been leaning on it without noticing.

"It's unlocked. Come in," she said.

Zinnia slowly unlatched the gate, then crept toward the girl. She got about three feet away, then stopped, not daring to disturb the ring of ants twisting around the other girl's feet.

The other girl held out her arm, palm facing up. An ant carried a large skin flake onto her hand, then dropped it onto the center of her palm. The flake melted and sizzled like butter into the girl's skin, becoming a bump like a burn scar, which sunk into her skin and disappeared.

Zinnia's eyes went wide. She took a step back, then another. "What...?"

A cloud drifted over the sunshine of the girl's smile.

"You're pollinating. I thought you knew."

"That's..."

"Pollen, yes. Not skin." she said, with a hint of sadness in her voice. She looked long and pityingly on Zinnia with her long-lashed brown eyes. "You're Zinnia, aren't you? They cut down your mother's home tree, so there was no one to teach you."

"Wait wait wait...there are *other* Home Trees? That's not just something in my head?" Everything had just turned upside down, and it made Zinnia more than a little dizzy.

"I'm Poppy," said the girl, "That's my birch in the corner of the yard. My mothers have neighbouring oak trees down in the glen. Your mother... she was a dryad, and so are you."

"My mother died of cancer," Zinnia said, but as she did, her mind flashed back to the photo album under her bed, to the yellowed article that Mama Moncton had given her when she'd been old enough to keep it safe. The picture, faded with age but still very clear, showed the last known photo of her mother, chained to a giant cottonwood tree on the site of the old mall. She had been an activist, they said, who had fought tooth and nail to save that tree. The revelation cascaded down around her like a drift of fall leaves: she had been actually been fighting for her own life.

"Cancer is often what they call it," said Poppy, "But it's more akin to limb rot than anything. Dryads don't last more than a year past the death of their Home Tree. They just... decay."

"And my father? Was he a dryad too? I never knew him."

Poppy giggled a little, but Zinnia could tell that she was trying not to for the sake of the situation.

"We're all the same gender. Our ancestors chose to appear female, because that is easiest. The only difference between us is that, in the right season of life, one of us becomes the pollinator, the other the pollinated. All dryads are capable of both things, in the right season."

Zinnia felt a thrill of fear run through her that she suspected only teenage boys usually knew. A knot formed in the pit of her stomach, and pulled on her ribcage.

"You're pregnant?"

What would they do? People heaped enough shame on teen moms as it was, but they would never believe that Poppy had been impregnated by a girl on top of it all, even if the explanation made any sense at all to humans...wait a minute, she was a human. Why was she thinking like this? And yet, Poppy's words tugged at her.

"I will be pregnant," Poppy replied, "But that is part of a different season. It will not happen the way you expect, but for now, you need to know that we are family."

The ants dispersed, gone back to the obscurity of the grass. Poppy came close to Zinnia, and with a thrill of energy arcing between them, she kissed her on the cheek.

"Come inside and meet my mothers," she said, "We have been waiting for you."

Poppy took Zinnia's hand, and, to her great surprise, she followed toward the house, where the smell of lunch drifted out of the open door and she could hear the sounds of music and laughter.

To Zombie Or Not To Zombie
Ira Nayman

"Mom! Dad's eye has fallen into the cereal again!"

"Left or right?"

"Umm...right."

"That's his good eye! Fish it out of the cereal and put it back in its socket!"

"Eww! Gross! I'm not doing that!"

Rebekah chugged out of the kitchen and into the dining room, muttering, "Fine! I'll do it myself! I have to do everything around here!"

Taking the spoon from her husband's compliant fingers, she fished around in the bowl on the table in front of him until she came out with an eyeball. Rebekah tenderly wrapped the eyeball in her apron and gently dried it off. Then, she put it up to the empty socket and, her brow furrowed with concentration, thought: Connect to the optic nerve. Connect to the optic nerve. Connect to the optic nerve, damn you! Connect to the optic nerve and stay connected to the optic nerve!

When Rebekah took her hand away, the eyeball stayed in the socket.

"Are we gonna have to go through this every morning?" Shoshana, 12, complained.

"You have to understand," Rebekah said, "your father is... going through changes..."

"Yeah," Izzy, 11, enthusiastically commented. "For one thing: HE'S DEAD!

"IZZY!" Rebekah responded. "Show some respect! He may be dead, but he's still your father – more or less – probably – as far as anybody can tell – anyway, he looks like your father, so that's good en –"

Ian moaned. It was a deep rumbling, which made it hard to understand what he was trying to say. Rebekah thought she made out the word, "Shuuuuuul," which would make sense, given that it was Saturday.

Could she risk taking Ian to synagogue in his…condition?

The Beth Emeth's Rabbi Schneerman might be okay with Ian's…current state of being. After all, he was the "hip" young Rabbi who was training to replace Rabbi Kvelman when he retired in January. Still, the fact that he didn't know that the word "hip" was no longer, well, hip gave Rebekah pause. Rabbi Kvelman, on the other hand, would undoubtedly use the knowledge of Ian's… unusual biological status as an excuse to tell the Golem story – he loved that cautionary tale so much, he told it whenever he had an excuse to (and, often, when he didn't), loved it even before he had gone near anybody who even remotely resembled one. Still, Ian's… altered state of physical dynamism posed no threat to the State of Israel, so Rabbi Kvelman might not have a problem with him.

No. If there was to be a problem, it would probably come from other members of the congregation. Eric Goldman, a lawyer, would want to know if Ian still paid taxes now that he was not, you know, strictly speaking, alive. Eric had no ulterior motive in asking this question, he would hasten to let you know, he was just… curious. Yeah. That's it. Curious. Shirley Suvenneman would want to know how Rebekah and Ian, oh, this is a little embarrassing, I know, but still, I have to ask, in the spirit of scientific enquiry, if nothing else, how the two of you, you know, did it. And, just to be clear, she would add that she's not talking about playing bridge! (So far, Ian slept on the couch. He had slept there more than once during the rough patches in their marriage when he was alive, so he knew the drill and didn't object to it now.) Esther Hanuman would want to know how such a thing was possible, I mean, it couldn't possibly be natural – perhaps it was a sign of the coming of the Moshiach. Not that she was afraid – she was ready to be judged, although can any of us say we are truly ready to be judged and, okay, maybe she was clearly not ready to be judged, and, if Ian's… you know was a sign that the Moshiach was coming, could he please, please, please, please, please judge her last so that she could have a little time to prepare?

Bathurst Manor was dripping with compassion. Really. They had to wash it off the streets every morning.

It wasn't that Ian was a stereotypical…person in a condition of no longer entirely deadness. His flesh wasn't rotting, for instance. It appeared to be functioning as normal – well, except for the parts that seemed to be missing (most notably the nail on his right thumb, a hole in his left knee and part of his right eye). As he always had, he smelled of vague strawberries (the fruit was vague, not his odor). He didn't hunger for human brains; he seemed content with Captain Commando cereal and the occasional raw steak.

Still, many members of the congregation had been to his funeral two weeks earlier, or brought drooping flowers to the shiva last week, or gave their condolences over the phone and explained why circumstances would not allow them to go to the funeral or the shiva. They knew Ian had died. Questions would be asked.

"Shuuuuuuuuuul!" Ian moaned. Rebekah frowned. Ian appeared much more eager to spend his Saturdays in prayer than he had when he was…not as you see him now. Maybe the experience had taught him something profound about the nature of existence. Or, maybe he was going through the motions in a sad parody of his previous life. *If only I had been more of a fan of George Romero movies*, Rebekah mused, *I might better understand what he's going through.*

"Mooooom!" Shoshana asked, "Do we have to go to shul?"

"Shuuuuuuul!" Ian moaned.

"It does seem to be what your father wants," Rebekah answered.

"Since when has that ever mattered?" Izzy complained.

"Since he died!" Rebekah shouted.

"Yeah, shul, that's not gonna be awkward," Shoshana pointed out.

This reminder seemed to have a calming effect on Rebekah. "Yes, there is that," she allowed. "Okay, maybe not this week."

"Shuuuuul!" Ian moaned.

"But, don't think you're getting out of anything," Rebekah scolded. "When you're done with breakfast, go up to your rooms and…pray or something!"

"Do you have lunch money?"

"No."

"Give it to me."

"Or, what?"

"I…I…I'll…disrupt your morphic field!"

That's what Izzy loved about Hebrew school: the bullies were so sophisticated.

"You wouldn't dare!"

"You know I don't make idle threats. My threats are very active – that's how they keep their figures."

"I – what?" Izzy was confused. Confused is not a useful reaction to a bully.

"Focus, my man, focus," Abraham ordered. "If you don't give me your lunch money, I will disrupt your morphic field."

"My what?"

"Morphic field."

"Is that…where we play soccer?"

Abraham hit his forehead with the palm of his hand. "On a morphic field? No!"

"Is that where negotiations between unions and management are supposed to take place?"

"Are you pretending to be stupid?" Abraham coldly asked.

"No, no, absolutely not!" Izzy insisted. "I really am stupid!"

"Your morphic field is what allows you to sense the things around you," Abraham explained. "Without it, you would not know if somebody was creeping up behind you."

"I don't know if people are creeping up on me now!"

"You have the ability, you just haven't developed it. Just like playing the piano. Or, ping pong. Or, tying a noose. Or, killing orcs in Dungeons and Dragons. Or, playing piano while killing orcs in Dungeons and Dragons. You see what I'm saying?"

"No."

Abraham sighed. "Look. Lunch is just about over. Why don't we just take it as a given that you are sufficiently intimidated to do whatever I tell you to do and you hand me your lunch money?"

Abraham was short, slightly built with a soft voice and thick glasses. Not your classic bully type. Yet, he could be very persuasive, especially in hallways away from the main classrooms in the synagogue. Izzy was putting his hand in his pocket when, completely out of the blue – not to mention out of character – he said: "If you don't leave me alone, my dad will kick your ass!"

"Interesting," Abraham replied, unexpectedly sanguine about a potential adult asskicking, "considering that your father died in a collision with a cigarette truck two months ago. Smoking obviously wasn't good for his health. Haw! Ha ha! But, seriously, despite the fact that you clearly have some entertainment value, I really just want your money. Now, before we have to go back to class."

"My dad's back!" Izzy insisted. "He's back, and if he kicked death's ass, you better believe he isn't afraid of any moraphic fields!"

"Morphic fields," Abraham corrected him. "Okay. Fine. Have it your way. Your dead dad is back."

"Damn straight."

"Meet me in the kiddy playground by the side of the shul after class."

"Damn – what?"

"Dead dads – that's not something you see every day. I figure it's gotta be worth a field trip."

Izzy realized that he may have gone too far. "Oh, no," he backtracked. "I'm not really supposed to – I mean, nobody's supposed to – here. Here. Take my lunch money." Izzy shoved his money in Abraham's direction.

"I will take this," Abraham intoned, "because of the principle involved. And, I will see you after class. Because of the curiousity involved."

"But, nobody's supposed to know!"

Abraham grinned. "It'll be our secret, then."

One afternoon learning the joys of the Hebrew language later, Izzy tried to quietly sneak away from the synagogue. Unfortunately, Abraham was waiting for him by the door opposite the door that let out to the kiddy playground.

"Fish are so predictable," Abraham philosophized.

"Not many surprises when all you do all day is swim in water," Izzy muttered.

"Show time, 'I See Dead People' boy!" Abraham exulted as he took Izzy's arm and led him off. The trip to Izzy's house took ten minutes. They made it in silence.

Izzy and Abraham watched Izzy's dad watch television through a window at the side of the house for a couple of minutes. "Your dad must be the most boring dead guy ever!" Abraham finally complained. "He doesn't do anything!"

"Yeah. Sorry about that," Izzy apologized. He didn't feel especially apologetic, but it was just a thing you did with the school bully.

Abraham took off his backpack and started rummaging around in it. "Open the window," he commanded.

"Why?"

"Yours not to wonder why," Abraham sagely told him. "Yours but to do or have your morphic field die."

Izzy opened the window.

Abraham took a straw out of his backpack.

"Aww, no!" Izzy groaned.

"Aww, yes!" Abraham exclaimed as he put the straw between his lips. He took careful aim and let loose a spitball that hit Ian in the side of the head.

"Owwwwwwwww!" Ian moaned. He raised his hand to where the spitball had hit him, promptly forgot why he had raised his hand to his head and let it slowly fall back into his lap.

"YES!" Abraham exulted. "Unofficial home room spitball champion three years running!"

"Okay," Izzy anxiously said. "You got him. Got him good. Now, I really think it's time to go!"

"Time to go?" Abraham laughed. "Seriously? Man, where's your entrepreneurial spirit?"

"I don't think this is a good –"

"Idea? You're right. This is not a good idea."

"Good. Then –"

"It's a great idea!" Abraham roared.

racystaceygrace: i can't believe my dad won't let me get a drath vader tattoo!

shonuff27: I know, eh?

racystaceygrace: dad's can be such a pain in the ass!

shonuff27: tell me about it!

    Shoshana sat on the bed in her room and listened to Herb Albert/Kate Bush mashups. She was surrounded by posters of the latest musical heartthrobs, some Montreal Canadiens (yeah, yeah, there's nothing traitorous about backing a winner) and even a couple of particle physicists (that Nils Bohr sure had sexy eyes!). For a girl her age, she had eclectic interests.
    She eagerly flipped to the inside back page of the day's Alternate Reality News Service Teen Journal. And, there it was!

Dear Amritsar,
    My dad is a zombie. Don't judge. Like most zombies, he doesn't have a great command of the language, but he could still tell me to do things like: "Diiiiiiiiiishes!" or "Rooooooom!" Do I have to listen?
    Shoshana from North York

Hey, Babe,
    There are two trains of thought in the burgeoning undead parenting movement. In the first, creatures that look and act more or less like a dead parent have to be given the benefit of the doubt. There is currently no way of knowing what goes on in a zombie's head: they are likely calculating how high to raise their arms to achieve the maximum frightening effect, but they could be on the verge of solving Lehmer's Mahler measure problem and just not have the capacity to articulate their calculations. Most zombie researches are prepared to split the difference; unfortunately for

you, this includes being able to order children to do the dishes, although there is some debate over whether it includes ordering them to clean their rooms.

The second approach, a little more nuanced, deals with the consciousness of the undead parent. Aside from an insatiable thirst for blood, your average vampire could be said to have all of his mental faculties; you would, therefore, be required to follow his parental orders (probably short of bloodletting, but since that has nothing to do with your question, I will leave the issue for another column). MRI scans have shown conclusively that zombies have diminished brain function – so diminished, in some cases that they make vegetables look like Nobel Prize winners! (You may have heard of "high functioning" zombies, but that mostly means that they pick up their feet when they walk rather than shamble.) In this way, whether or not you have to listen to your undead parent depends on the degree of consciousness she could be said to attain in her current state.

Keep in mind, though, that this approach is highly controversial. What happens when one parent is possessed by the malevolent spirit of the dead other parent? Do both parents have sufficient volition to require that their commands to be followed? If not, how can you determine which parent is telling you what to do at any given time, and, therefore, which orders to follow and which to ignore? Until psychologists, Ghostbusters and descendants of van Helsing come to some agreement on this issue, the first approach will remain the only viable one.

So, sorry, but it would appear that, to be on the safe side you still have to clean your room. Or, roooooom.

Amritsar went on to answer a question about whether or not a human should share her toothbrush when her Ferenghi boyfriend sleeps over, which didn't interest Shoshana at all. She threw the copy of The Alternate Reality News Service Teen Journal to the ground; it hadn't been very helpful!

• • •

Somebody knocked on the door. Rebekah was watching CBC Newsworld to see if the zombie apocalypse had started and what advice Peter Mansbridge had for dealing with it. Oil prices were on the rise again. A politician said something offensive to somebody and gave an apology which really didn't apologize for it, which was fine because nobody who had been offended was willing to accept it. A riot at Queen's Park was averted when a wall of water appeared between two groups of opposed protestors. Nothing new there. Ian was mesmerized by the television, to the point where a thin line of drool rolled out of his mouth. Nothing new there, either.

Rebekah opened the door to find a thirtysomething man with a weaselly face whose clothing looked like a two year-olds' finger painting gone horribly, horribly wrong.

"Antonio?" she asked/accused. Accusked.

"Hey, Beks," Antonio Van der Whall greeted her.

"What are you doing here?" Rebekah accusked him. There was definite accuskation in her voice.

"Oh, you know," he said with a breezy wave of his hand. "Fran heard from Aunt Queenie who heard from her Cousin Lorna who heard from her brother Aaron who heard from his niece Gila who heard from her son Abraham that something strange might be going on with Ian. So, I thought I'd just pop –"

"Ian?" Rebekah asked, holding tightly to the door. "Nothing strange is going on with –"

"I spoke to his left armpit on the way over," Van der Whall stopped her. "I know the atoms in his body did their best to reincorporealize – if that's a word, and, if not, it is now – him a week and a half or so after he died. Can I come in and see him?"

Rebekah let go of her death grip on the door and let Van der Whall pass. She followed him as he made his way to the den. Van der Whall considered Ian for a couple of minutes. When it appeared that Ian was content to completely ignore him, Van der Whall quietly said, "Ian?"

Ian looked at him for a few seconds, head gently bobbing, before saying, "Tooooooooooo!"

"Close enough," Van der Whall smiled. Turning to Rebekah,

he commented, "The atoms really did a remarkable job, all things considered. Did you know –"

"Antonio, what are you talking about?" Rebekah cut him off. "What do you mean, you spoke to Ian's armpit on the way down, and what's all this talk of his atoms?"

Van der Whall sighed. His sigh said: Must I explain this once again. I mean, seriously, don't you get news in the suburbs? It's not like North York is Siberia – well, other than the frozen state of mind, in any case. It's been over 15 years since the Singularity made all matter in the universe conscious at all levels of organization – it was in all the papers! And, it's not like matter isn't willing to explain itself, either. No, drop into the Quantum Entanglement Dimension – where matter communicates instantaneously regardless of distance – some time and you'll see – you can't get newly conscious matter to shut up! I mean, okay, I know that people just want to get on with their lives, but you're my family – well, okay, Frances' family, but she's the love of my life, so that makes you practically my family – so, given the whole familiness of our relationship, how could you not know that I am, if I do say so myself – and I do – the foremost object psychologist in the world? HOW COULD YOU NOT KNOW ABOUT ME?

Seeing the incomprehension on Rebekah's face, Van der Whall realized that she didn't speak sigh language. So, he repeated himself. In English. With 87% less snark.

After he had finished, Rebekah took a couple of minutes to process what he had told her. "How could I not have known this?" she asked.

Van der Whall bit his tongue and replied, "You've been busy with your family..."

"So, what exactly happened?"

"Well, as best as I have been able to piece together," Van der Whall took a deep breath, "the grief that you and the children were feeling during the shiva –"

"Iiiiiiiivaaaaa," Ian moaned.

"Yes, Ian, shiva. Your grief was heard by the atoms in his dead body through the Quantum Entanglement Dimension. They discussed it among themselves, and decided to reincorporealize –

see, the word is growing on you, don't try to deny it – they decided to bring him back to life. There were only two problems with their plan. One: not all of his body parts agreed to return to him – some of them had already become part of the earth or the air or other things you could imagine if you thought about a body decomposing in the ground but you probably shouldn't so forget I mentioned it. So, some parts of his body might be missing. Two: atoms are good with structure, but not that great with process. In other words, they could recreate his brain but they couldn't recreate his thoughts –"

"Thooooooooots," Ian moaned.

"Precisely. So, you're left with a moaning, drooling, shambler of a husband. Still, give them credit, though – it's amazing that they got this much right!"

"As best as you have been able to piece together?"

"I came the moment I heard. If I had known sooner –"

Rebekah held up her hand. "Thanks for the pedantic explanation. So, what now?"

"Now," Van der Whall stated, slightly hurt. Being an academic, he shouldn't have cared about the accusation of pedantry – the truth need never concern itself with presentation style – but for some reason he did. "I can explain to Ian's body that it is actually making things worse, that, really, you and your family should be allowed to grieve and get on with your lives, and reincorporealizing – notice how I added a new formation of my new word, there? Cool what you can do with the language, isn't it? – reincorporealizing his body has made that much harder for you. I'm sure that the atoms will see reason and return to the ground where they belong."

"I don't know," Rebekah demurred. "I think Ian's presence has actually helped us."

"You do?"

"I was a mess after the accident," she explained. "I couldn't cook, the house was filthy, I couldn't even think about going back to work. The kids were in really bad shape, too. Ian's return calmed us all down, made things easier for us. Ian –"

"Beks," Van der Whall interrupted her. "You know how I hate cliches?"

"Your reputation for it in the family is legendary."

"So, you know how much what I'm about to say will pain me."

"I can get you an aspirin if it would help."

"Okay, then," Van der Whall took a deep breath. "The man sitting on the couch may look like your husband, but he's not. Your husband is dead and you will never get him back."

"That didn't seem so hard."

"I feel faint."

"Shall I get some smelling salts?"

"It'll pass."

"Good. Then, get out."

"I'm sorry?"

"Oooooowt," Ian moaned.

Rebekah rose. Out of reflex, Van der Whall rose as well. "I'll think about what you've said," she told him as she took his arm, "and I'll let you know what my decision is."

"But…but…" Van der Whall sputtered as Rebekah led him out of the den and towards the front door, "there will be questions. Complications. Problems. You have no idea what you're getting yourself into!"

"I thought you hated cliches," Rebekah pointed out as she opened the front door and guided Van der Whall through it.

"Sometimes," Van der Whall hotly stated, "you have to speak in language people will understand!"

"I know the feeling," Rebekah angrily responded. Her voice rising, she added: "Don't call us, we'll call you!" and slammed the door in his face.

Even before the sound stopped reverberating in her ears, she regretted it. He was only trying to help. In an irritating, meddlesome, "I know more about the universe than you ever will, so why don't we just agree that I'm right?" superior way, mind you. Still, he meant well, right? Rebekah decided that she liked Van der Whall's good intentions better when they were on the other side of the city.

By the time she got back to the den, she was angry with him all over again.

Before she could even register what was on television, there was another knock on the door. Rebekah strode through the house, threw open the door and began to shout, "Antonio, you always were a pri –" She stopped when she saw that it wasn't Van der Whall standing on the porch, that it was, in fact, a short, dry old man with a pencil moustache holding a briefcase that looked like it contained a lot of pencils.

"Oh, I am sorry," Rebekah flustered. "I thought –"

"Not to worry," the man assured her. "I get a lot of that. Mrs. Neuman?"

"Neiman."

"Naiman?"

"Neiman."

"Mrs. Ian Naiman?"

"No, Mrs. Ian Neiman."

"Close enough. Abercrombie. Monrovia."

"What can I do for you, Mister Monrovia?"

"Abercrombie."

"Sorry?"

"Mister Abercrombie."

"Maybe we should start again."

"Fair enough. Would you like to close the door so that I can knock on it again?"

"That won't be necessary. If you could just introduce yourself…"

"My name is Monrovia Abercrombie."

"It must be hard, going through life with such an ambiguous name."

"What?"

"What do you want?"

"Mister Abercrombie."

"Whoever you are."

"Ah. Yes. I'm a private investigator in the employ of Aetna Proaxial, Insurers at Medium to Large, the company that issued the policy on your late husband. I'm sorry I came on such short notice, but every time I called, the person who picked up the phone moaned, 'Looooooooow!' at me!"

Rebekah shifted uncomfortably on her feet. "Yes, well, I really must get that glitch looked after."

"In any case, we examined your claim last week…" Abercrombie continued.

"That's right. My husband died. Three weeks ago."

"Only, I'm hearing rumours that people have seen him walking around the neighbourhood."

Rebekah sighed. "I try to keep him in the house, but Ian has a mind of his own. So to speak."

Abercrombie looked surprised. "So, you're admitting that your husband is…still with us?"

"Hard to deny if he's getting loose."

"So, you'll understand if Aetna Proaxial denies your claim."

"Like hell I will! My husband died three weeks ago!"

"But, people have seen him –"

"HE CAME BACK!"

Abercrombie looked at Rebekah with a distinct lack of comprehension. In fact, he couldn't have had a less comprehensive expression if he had just sat down to complete a grade 12 French literature exam. So, he did what anybody in his position would do: after a suitable silence, he repeated back the last thing that had been said to him, only this time in the form of a question. "He came back?"

"Yes."

"From the dead?"

"That's right."

"How…" the man groped for a response, "how am I supposed to respond to this?"

"Does your company offer zombie apocalypse insurance?"

"Of course."

"You might want to reconsider!"

Rebekah slammed the door for the second time in as many porch conversations. Insurance investigators! This time, her feelings were not mixed.

. . .

Yutz' Deli has stood on Bathurst Street for over 70 years. And, just like any senior citizen, it could use a new coat of paint and, if we're being completely honest, it's one bulb short of being properly lit. Still, it makes the best liver and onions in town, and, these days, that's nothing to sneeze at (especially since its clientele is generally older than the building itself and prone to catch colds).

The Deli was run by Andrei Plutz, a distant cousin of Yaakov Yutz, its founder. Plutz, a big bear of a man with a tattoo of a woman on his arm that was PG below his elbow and R above it, spoke with a Russian accent even though he had been born in Scarborough. "Is how I was raised," he would explain with a shrug if anybody ever asked him about it, which nobody ever did because of the whole big bear of a man with a variably rated tattoo thing.

Rebekah worked at Yutz' Deli three days a week. She had started soon after she and Ian had been married, taking time off only during her pregnancies and the Festival of Festivals (which she refused to call by its new name because of a TIFF between her and head programm – dammit!). The plan was for Rebekah to become a full time mom when Ian's dentistry business took off. Unfortunately, family dentistry is a viciously competitive field, and he didn't live long enough to establish himself.

Rebekah sighed as she wiped down a table in the Deli. Truth be told, she hadn't wanted to stop working, but she wasn't thrilled about continuing to work under these circumstances, either. Rebekah was –

"You will please to check the roast beef, yes?"

"Has a customer asked for a roast beef sandwich?"

"No."

"Why do you want me to check it, then?"

"Oh, um," Andrei shifted his considerable bulk nervously. "To see if there is enough. Or, if I should put a new roast on the spit, maybe."

Rebekah looked across the room from the table she was wiping down to the counter next to the cash register, where the roast beef stood on a vertical spit for the viewing pleasure of customers. "Looks like there's plenty," she commented.

"Looks can deceiving," Andrei advised. "Look from behind

counter, please."

"Is that really necessary?"

"Please."

Rebekah left her schmatta on the table and went to the counter. At first, she didn't see what all the fuss was about. "It looks fine," she told Andrei.

"Look closer," he insisted.

Looking closer, she noticed that there was a message carved into the dark side of the roast beef (the side that wasn't facing the public). The message was: "Im hare for you." The Deli owner/manager watched her from the other side of the counter.

"Mister Plutz?"

"Please, call me Andrei."

"What is this supposed to be?"

"Is message of support."

"Im hare for you? You know rabbit isn't kosher."

"What? Here!"

"You want to serve rabbit here?"

"No, no! Is 'here.' Word is 'here.' I am here for you!"

"That's not what it says."

"Carving knife is imprecise tool. I am here for you is what I meant!"

"Oh, Mister Plutz!"

"Please, call me Andrei."

"That's very sweet of you, but –"

"Is too soon?"

"Well, no, it's not that, exactly…"

"You need big strong man in house, now that husband is gone, yes?"

"The thing is, Mister Plutz, Ian isn't really gone."

"I understand he is around in spirit (and, please, call me Andrei)."

"No. He is not around in spirit. He really is back at home, sitting on the couch, eating cereal and watching commentary on the 1972 Canada-Russia hockey showdown."

"Must be grief is talking."

"Not really. I mean, it was a close thing, but we eventually did win the Canada-Russia tournament."

"Forgive me, dear woman, for being so blunt, but husband is kaput."

"No. He came back."

"Sorrow is making you see things! It is too soon for working. You should go home."

"But, Mister Plutz –"

"Please, call me Andrei."

"I need the money!"

"I pay you anyway. Paid grief leave."

"Really?"

Andrei looked around the mostly empty deli. "I think I can handle dinner rush," he commented.

Rebekah considered for a moment. Mister Plutz was being awfully kind to her – she might say understanding if he had actually understood what was happening in her life. And, aside from a rumoured R-rated tattoo, he was an attractive man for his age (as long as you didn't think about using a machette to cut through the forest of hair on his chest – too late!). And, he was clearly a good provider (don't let the empty tables fool you – the Deli made a fortune on take-out orders). An objective observer might say that Rebekah was flattered by Mister' Plutz attention, had Heisenberg pretty much demolished the concept. A pushy objective observer might give Heisenberg the finger and conclude that she was interested in Mister Plutz. Under the circumstances, Rebekah could see only one reasonable course of action.

She went home early.

• • •

A dozen kids were lined up at the side of the house. They were joking and laughing or talking to their friends on their cellphones or playing Angry Reptiles on their PDAs, but they were all there with one goal in mind: to throw spitballs at the dead guy. At a dollar a pop. And, the best part? They had to supply their own straws and wads of paper!

"Okay, okay," Abraham loudly commanded, "stop pushing!

Everybody in line will get their turn. Hey! Yes, I'm talking to you! If I see you push the person in front of you one more time, you're outta here!"

"I'll get my money back, though, right?" the redheaded kid Abraham had singled out asked.

"Wadd I tell you?" Abraham shouted. "No refunds! Whaddya think this is – Yorkdale?"

"Hey! At least I got my iPhone at Yorkdale!" somebody in the line pointed out.

"Who said that?" Abraham, accusatorily looking up and down the line, screamed. "I dare the person who said that to say it to my face! What? Too chicken? Come on, you chicken! Make that crack about your iPhone to – oh! That reminds me…" Abraham took out his cellphone and started taking pictures of the line.

Izzy, aghast, asked, "What are you doing?"

"For the Twitter feed," Abraham explained.

"The what?" Izzy screeched.

"If we want to build volume," Abraham calmly told him, "we have to promote the business using social media. Common sense, really."

"But, we don't want to build volume!" Izzy hissed. "We already have enough volume! Too much volume!"

"That's the problem with this country," Abraham stated. "Entrepreneurs are no longer willing to take risks."

"We're going to get caught!"

"Why would we get caught? We know what hours your mother wor –"

Izzy and Abraham's heads jerked to the side when they heard the family jeep pull up in the driveway.

"Who is that?"

"My mother!"

"You told me she wouldn't be back before eight."

"We're doomed!"

"We had an agreement, mister!"

"We're doomed! We're doomed! We're doomed!" Izzy chanted, rocking gently on his heels.

"Listen up, everybody!" Abraham shouted as a car door

could be heard slamming shut. "Code Trojan Horse! You hear me? CODE TROJAN HORSE! NOW!"

Everybody pocketed their straws and took out a baseball glove just as Rebekah ducked her head over the fence to the side of the house.

"Hello, boys," she greeted.

"Hello, Mrs. Neiman," they responded. More or less. In unison. Give or take.

"What are you doing?" Rebekah asked.

"Just playing a little ball," Abraham told her.

"Who has the ball?"

The boys looked around at each other, each hoping that somebody else had an answer. After a few seconds, Abraham took a ball out of his pocket and dully responded, "Oh. Here it is."

Rebekah looked them over. "Hmm… I see eleven boys and seven catchers mitts. What kind of a game are you boys playing, here?"

Abraham shrugged. "J. P. Arencibia is our favourite player."

"Un hunh." Rebekah looked skeptical. "Why are you playing on the side of the house? Wouldn't it be roomier to play in the back yard?"

"We were, uhh, warming up, here," Abraham knew how lame he sounded, but for the sake of the enterprise he felt obligated to see the argument through to its conclusion. "We were planning on going into the back as we were ready. You know. For the room."

"Uh hunh. Why is Sammy holding a straw?"

All eyes turned to the chubby kid at the head of the line. Abraham was so stunned, he couldn't even come up with a lame retort, much less a clever one. He pocketed the tennis ball (it wasn't even a baseball, not that it mattered now).

Rebekah looked around, piecing things together. Eventually, she said, "Go home, boys." The quietness of her voice was like a whip. The yard emptied at sub-sonic speed (barely), leaving just Izzy and his mother.

"Let's go in," Rebekah told him. "This has gone too far."

"Okay."

"And, Izzy?"

"Yeah?"
"Close the window."

• • •

Rebekah was busy at the stove. As she had requested, Izzy and Shoshana were sitting at the kitchen table. "Children," she said lightly over her shoulder, "we need to talk."

Shoshana rolled her eyes. Rebekah was tempted to respond, "I heard that," but that would not help create the atmosphere she felt was necessary for what the family needed to hash out, so, instead, she said, "I'm making cocoa."

"Oh oh." Shoshana responded.

"Oh oh?"

"You only make cocoa when you want to talk to us about something 'difficult,'" Izzy explained.

"That's not true!" Rebekah protested.

"We call it 'Mom's Oh Oh Cocoa,'" Shoshana told her.

"But –"

"That's not a bad thing," Izzy argued. "Mom's Oh Oh Cocoa's Facebook fan page has 1,237 likes."

Rebekah stopped for a moment. "Is that good?" she asked.

"So so," Izzy told her. "If I wasn't so busy with school, I could post more to the page – maybe raise your numbers. Still, Mom's Oh Oh Cocoa –"

"Oooooooh," Ian moaned from the den. All conversation in the kitchen stopped while the sentient family members tried to figure out if he was asking for cocoa or trying to tell them that he would like the Mom's Oh Oh Cocoa fan page.

"Okay," Rebekah finally said. "Well. We can talk about that some other time. I really wanted to talk to you about –" Just then, the kettle whistled. "Give me one second…"

Shoshana and Izzy stifled giggles as their mother poured the hot water into their mugs. Still, they took their cocoa gratefully and drank eagerly.

Rebekah started again: "We need to talk about your father."

"You mean, that creepy thing on the couch?" Shoshana

asked.

"Hey!" Izzy barked.

"He's not our father!" Shoshana barked back. "I remember our father when he was really our father! He used to try and teach me how to fix a leaky pipe – and he didn't even know! Mostly, we mopped up the spill. But…but – we used to go to Blue Jays games together, even though he could never quite get the hang of the infield fly rule. He used to take us both to the movies –"

"If I never see Despicable Me again…" Izzy muttered.

"Okay, nine times may have been excessive," Shoshana allowed. "But, dad really loved that movie, and, anyway, minions."

"Minions," Izzy agreed.

"Anyway," Shoshana continued, "the point is that that thing sitting on the couch looks like dad – with a piece or two missing – but he doesn't act like dad. There's no dad there."

"I know," Rebekah, agreed. Then, she took a deep breath and said: "Your Uncle Antonio says he can help your father go back to his final resting place."

"Talk about creepy," Izzy said.

"Hey!" Shoshana protested.

"Well, he is!" Izzy insisted. "He thinks he can talk to plants and animals – one time, he tried to tell me what a great conversation he had with his kitchen chair. 'You can learn a lot from an experienced piece of furniture,' he told me. 'They can be very deep.' Tell me that's not creepy!"

"He showed me how to talk to objects, once," Shoshana insisted. "Everything he says is true!"

"Gimme that!" Izzy exclaimed, grabbing for her mug. "You don't deserve Mom's Oh Oh Cocoa!"

"Children, enough!" Rebekah shouted, rubbing her aching forehead. She was an attractive woman in her mid-30s, but she frowned so often she was already beginning to develop Grand Canyonal wrinkles. "We can't go on like this."

"Because dad will try to eat our brains?" Izzy asked, more curious than scared.

"No, dad will not try to eat anybody's brains," Rebekah wearily responded.

"See?" Shoshana went back to the well one last time. "Whatever is out there isn't even a proper zombie!"

"We need closure on Ian's death," Rebekah stated. "Antonio is right – we need to get on with our lives, and we can't do that while he's sitting on the couch. Do you understand?"

The children agreed.

After the cocoa, Rebekah sent them to their rooms and walked into the den. She watched Ian watching television. She fondly remembered how awkward he was when they first started dating; dropping the turkey on her father's head on Rosh Hashanah was especially problematic, although it did show a remarkable dexterity on Ian's part. Rebekah found this endearing. Some people would have chalked it up to the pot that they were both experimenting with at the time, but the only effect it ever had on Ian was to make him sound like Don Cherry.

Over time, Ian seemed to grow into himself. At the Rosh Hashanah dinner after Shoshana was born, he only dropped the noodle pudding on her father's head. Progress!

She could not deny that he was good with the children. Rebekah smiled at her memory of the time Ian, just establishing his dental practice, brought home a three foot tall molar – the children, barely larger than the tooth itself, got hours of enjoyment placing the attachments that illustrated various diseases on the molar. Say what you will about the parenting technique, but neither Shoshana nor Izzy had ever had a single cavity.

She positively guffawed at Ian's attempt to develop a goatee.

The marriage wasn't all fun and games, of course. There were the arguments about money. And, there were the arguments about whether plush toys were better for the environment than building blocks. And, inevitably, there were the arguments over whether Aunt Minnie should be allowed to stay the night after all of the horrible things she said about Ian's anaesthetic administering technique. Funny how none of it seemed to matter now. Well, none of it except the plush toys versus the building blocks argument – the ongoing assault on the environment caused by children's toys is an important issue for our children's future!

When times were good, though, times were very good. The

trip they made to Hollywood is etched upon her mind. No, wait – that was a song. They only actually made it to her cousin Remy's loft in Hoboken. Izzy was conceived under the watchful eye of black and white 1950s atomic mutant horror movie posters. In their youthful joy, the couple thought it was all very post-Spockian.

Rebekah walked over to Ian and affectionately kissed him on the top of the head. "Ruuuuuuuuer?" he moaned. "Ruuer," she replied. Then, she picked up the phone and dialled the first eight numbers.

"Hey, Beks!" Van der Whall greeted her. "Glad you decided to call."

"The phone didn't start to ring," Rebekah said. "In fact, I didn't finish dialling. What the hell, Antonio?"

"Oh, I asked your phone to contact me through the QED if it looked like you were trying to call me," Van der Whall explained. "I gave it my number – I figured that by the time you got the eighth number correct, you couldn't be phoning anybody else."

"But, you didn't even pick up."

"Well, no. Technically, I'm talking to your phone through the QED. Would you rather I got on the phone at my end? Some people find crackling static so comforting…"

"Uhh, no, that's fine."

"Good. So. Ready to admit that I was right?"

"As a matter of fact –"

"It's okay. I usually am. Right, I mean…"

Rebekah could feel her cheeks flushing with anger. "Look –" she started.

"Oh, just say, 'You were right, Tonio,'" Van der Whall cut her off, "and we can get on to more important matters. Like, what we're going to do now that we've agreed that I was right."

"YOU DON'T MAKE IT EASY!"

"Well, of course I don't make it easy. If everything in life was easy, how would anybody learn anything?"

"Okay. Fine. You were right," Rebekah muttered.

"Thank you. So, what shall we do now?"

"Can you come over and convince Ian to go back to being dead?"

"Absolutely. Only, I'll have to make it quick. I just heard from my uncle Philboyd that his brother Kane had heard from his cousin Winthrop who had heard from his aunt Jemimah that her recently deceased step-son was behaving very strangely. I need to check this out – we may have a slower-than-usual-motion apocalypse on our hands!"

Ghosts In My Hair
Elizabeth Hirst

Melanie had sported the bob for four years running, and it had to go. The whole short hair thing was just a hangover from high school anyway, when she did a lot of sports and kept away from boys.

As she sat in her afternoon lecture, doodling different hairdos, Melanie hatched out a Mohawk, an undercut, a perm. . . none of them made the sparks fly.

Then, after class, Kelly caught up to her, with his long, black metal hair, thin goatee and 80s throwback shirt. That's when sparks flew. When she got near, she smelled the sweet spice of his cologne and her breath got short for a moment. His eyes and his smile made everything else fuzzy.

"Hey," she said, pointing to the bathroom, "Can I have a minute?"

"Be my guest," he said, smiling as if he found even this mundane activity vaguely amusing.

Melanie gave him a goofy grin, and then walked into the Men's room. Oops.

After Melanie emerged, still red-faced, from the proper lavatory, Kelly invited her for a bite to eat in their favourite courtyard. The University was full of courtyards, but this one was long and thin, walled in by four storey buildings on either side, accessible only from the basement, or the back of the building. Up top, the sky, and on the ground, a few trees and benches where the cafeteria workers came out occasionally to smoke. In between, nothing but long library windows sealed against winter. The perfect place to talk – maybe not to make out, but definitely to talk.

Melanie's fingers trembled slightly as she unwrapped her ham and cheese. The damp air seeped through her windbreaker, touching her skin with a slight chill.

"I'm sorry about the other night," said Kelly, "I shouldn't

have put pressure on you without knowing where you stood."

"You already knew where I stood. I'm waiting until marriage," Melanie replied, with as firm a tone as possible without sounding angry.

He fixed her with brown eyes so dark and doe-like that it was impossible to tell the pupil from the iris. It was simultaneously aggravating and exciting that he seemed to look right into her and read what was there. He said, "You say that, but I feel like something has changed since then."

"I can want to, and not act on it. That's all you saw in my face. I didn't hide anything from you, ever. If you don't like the terms of our relationship, you can date other people," Melanie replied, proud of the way she pushed the sound of tears from her voice and slowly relaxed the ache of her contracting throat. You had to stay strong with men. Otherwise they'd walk all over you. In relationships, there might be many roads to love, but there was only one road to respect. And she was taking it.

He pulled her in for a warm, sweat-shirty hug. Oh no. Her eyes welled, and she breathed deep until everything receded again. "Yeah, I get that," he said, "But I feel like we have something special."

Melanie, in three seconds of panicked thought, scanned her brain for an answer – any answer. A sacrificial lamb. Then a series of pen strokes hit her brain like lightning – pen strokes from the doodles on her notes.

"We do have something special," she said, "and I'll prove it to you. What kind of hair do you find sexiest?"

"I like long hair...as long as possible. Why?"

"Then I'll grow my hair out, just for you. And...and when it's done," she said, heart fluttering, blushing at her boldness, "We'll talk about it again. How about that?"

His heavy, black eyebrows sank as he studied her. For a moment, she thought he would call bullshit. She would have called bullshit. She knew he knew it was bullshit, even, but for some reason, he let her keep it up. Mr. Big-time Hardcore Rocker had a soft spot.

"Fine. Take four months. Grow your hair out. Until then, I'll let it ride."

Hallelujah, Melanie thought to herself, I've just been saved.

Melanie stepped out of the shower. She towelled off, then brushed the tangles out of her shoulder-length tresses. Three months into her hair growing expedition and she was finally beginning to see results. She rummaged through a vanity drawer and pulled out her hairdryer. She wanted her hair to be silky-soft perfection for the concert tonight, wanted Kelly to run his fingers through it in a quiet moment, sending her scalp off into cascades of tingles.

Click. Her hair kicked back like mermaid fins, like dancers' legs, like Pandora's demons loosed from the chest. The wind howled from the hairdryer like a child crying lost in a gale…wait…that was a weird noise for a hairdryer to make.

Your secrets live in here… something whispered. Shaking, she turned the hairdryer off for a moment. No dents in the end piece, no loose elements. She turned it on, aimed it at the sink, and listened. Nothing. She raised it to her hair again. Definitely something. The screaming of a soul trapped in hell.

We're going to tell him everything!

Melanie put the hairdryer down, her eyes wide as saucers, and picked up a towel. Nothing like the old-fashioned method.

They walked back from the train station, across overpasses and through tunnels, and finally, up the long hill to the cluster of apartment buildings surrounding the school. Reflections of streetlights shimmered in the last of the late fall rains, and the smell of fallen leaves and old motor oil wafted out of the gutters. Although it was chilly, Melanie undid her jacket as they passed the first bridge.

She had been the best-dressed girl in the room. Kelly hadn't been able to take his eyes, or his hands, off her. They had shared a slow dance to his favourite song. She wanted that moment to last for a lifetime. She wanted this date to last for a lifetime. No expectations, no sacrifices…just the stars, the music, and the moment. She got ahead of Kelly, to the corners, empty now in the dead of night. She looked up at the stars, opened her arms, and spun.

"Let's just stay out here all night," she said, "It'll all be ours, just for a few hours."

Kelly chuckled.

"But we'd get all damp after a while. Let's just go home and get warm," he said, with a twinkle in his eye. For a moment, Melanie studied Kelly, and he studied her, across the distance of three sidewalk segments. Her pulse raced.

"You're terrible," she said, half-turning her back and holding out a hand. He grabbed the hand, pulled her into his arms and kissed her hard.

Standing outside of Melanie's building, they faced one another, electricity running between their entwined fingers like uninsulated wires. A wind skirted the foundations of the building, rushing up from beneath them both and pushing Melanie's hair into the air. It howled, the same lonely sound as she had heard coming from her hairdryer earlier that evening. Only...the sound wasn't coming from the wind...it was coming from her hair.

Kelly backed off a bit, his fingertips brushing hers as he pulled away. She held her hands out, still, wanting him to come back. His eyes had left hers. He now looked above her head, where her hair swirled in the wind.

"Melanie, what's going on? There's...a face...in your hair," he said.

"What? Okay, you've breathed something in at the concert, and you're freaking out. Just calm down."

As she said this, the wind died down, and she felt her hair hit her shoulders. Kelly bent over and frowned like he was going to be sick. "Shit. I better get home and get some rest," he said.

"Are you going to be okay?"

"Yeah, I'll be fine. I'll see you tomorrow."

Melanie nodded and headed for the door. He called out to her one more time, now a hunched-over shadow blending in with the waving trees on the darkened street.

"Melanie? I love you."

Melanie pulled her jacket closer to her heart.

"I love you too. Be safe."

When he had gone, and she fitted her key into the lock, another gust of wind blew up. A voice, right by her ear, hissed, *Whore.*

Stay inside. That would be the formula from now on. Stay out of the wind when Kelly was around. It could be months before he even noticed anything was wrong. Melanie stayed in her apartment as much as possible as the winds of late fall closed in, afraid of what the wind through her hair would say, and to whom. She felt her hair moving, at night, shifting and tickling her, agitating her until she lay sweaty and worn out, unable to sleep. Three days earlier, she had pulled some leftover pizza out of the fridge, and peeled the cheese off the top, to find three, long, hairs sitting on top of the tomato sauce. She had eaten nothing but individually packaged foods ever since. She was starving, and thirsty.

But he still hadn't heard it talk. He was coming over for a movie night tonight; Melanie had been sure to close every window, to stopper every door frame. An hour before his arrival, her room felt so unbearably stuffy that she had to have some fresh air. She burst out onto the balcony, relishing the cool breeze on her cheeks. She went to the railing and rested her elbows on it, watching the last of the students trickling past from evening classes.

A figure in a striped retro revival dress and a pea coat emerged from the forest across the street. She had long, dark, glossy hair, a pale, heart-shaped face and red rose lips. Something stirred deep inside Melanie, against her will and decidedly against her conscience. Her blowing hair pulled out in all directions.

She's dangerous! She wants to fuck you! It yelled, *Don't trust her!*

Melanie screamed and clamped her hands over her head. Rather than settling, her hair flew up and around her wrists, pinning them in place. She struggled against her bonds, but her hair held firm. She would have yanked it all out then and there, if she'd had the strength.

You like this, don't you? It said, *Whore. Filth. I'm telling everyone.*

Melanie screamed again and her hair finally let go, slipping away from her hands like silk, like nothing had ever held it in place. She rushed inside, collapsed on the couch and cried until nothing was left inside her but ache and shame.

Kelly found her in the same state, curled up and red-eyed in her pajamas, and for once she didn't care.

"What's wrong, Melanie?" he said, coming to sit by her.

"I'm cutting my hair," she said.

His face darkened. His black brows hovered like storm clouds over his eyes.

"I knew it. I knew you would do this."

Melanie realized in a flash what Kelly meant.

"No, that's not what I meant..."

"Then we're going to have sex? Tonight? How about next week? Ten years from now?"

"Kelly..." Melanie croaked, so out of tears, but not out of pain, apparently. A flash of lightning illuminated the sky outside and thunder rumbled in the distance.

"My friends told me not to bother. I guess I should have listened," Kelly said. He got up from the couch like someone who has just woken up from a long sleep, grabbed his coat and made for the door. "I've got to go and do some thinking, Melanie. I'll see you around."

The door shut behind him, and a floodgate opened somewhere inside Melanie. A black floodgate, holding back a million years of ash and rotting fur and blackened cats' teeth. Her hands went, clawed, to her forehead, and her eyes went wide.

"No," she said quietly, and then, louder, until she was yelling it, screaming it, pulling on her outdoor clothes without a thought to her bloody hair. She raced down the fire escape to the ground floor and shoved the door. The wind pulled it the rest of the way, slamming it against the side of the building. Rain blew sideways. Leaves whipped by. She stepped down into two inches of muck. She raced around to the front of the building, her hair screaming obscenities out behind her.

He's never going to love you. You know what men do to bisexual girls? The ones who want to be tied up? Use them and leave. You'll do anything. You're cheap.

He was still there, a shadow, as before, bending over the front door of a taxi.

"Kelly!" She yelled, and he stood up. The taxi drove away without him. She ran to Kelly, stood before him. In the garish flourescent light, he stared at her hair, making its faces and spreading its legs. She let him.

Her hair, and the wind, and the ghosts told him everything. He listened, the rain soaking into his hoodie. To her growing astonishment, he didn't look angry, or afraid. Her hair flew and swirled and pulled until finally, as lightning struck the ground behind them, in the flash of light it all detached, and floated into the whirlwind growing around her. The wind carried it all away, leaving her cold, damp, messy...and bald. She shivered and wrapped her arms around herself. Another set of arms wrapped around her, too.

"I'm ugly," she said, without shock, resigned to the fact at last.

Kelly kissed her forehead. "You're perfect. Come on upstairs."

Melanie took him upstairs, and, baldly, they made love.

Dakota Is A Dryad's Name
Elizabeth Hirst

Dakota emerged onto gravel. He reeled at the size of the dark blue sky, the black forest lining the road. Nowhere to get a bus schedule, or ask directions. He was going to explode. He was going to collapse. He'd catch a ride back home. Alberta to Toronto…his Mom had done it.

"Dakota is a girl's name!" they'd chanted, all summer. The man at the foundation had promised him food, friends and fun, a summer with new kids, kids not from his neighbourhood…but how did you have fun when you were bad at everything? The other kids practised sports at home. Dakota delivered fliers.

A logging truck rocketed past him, throwing off branches. Something reflective glinted in its headlights. No, the truck was gone, so what glowed gold from the center line?

Dakota inched out onto the asphalt. When no trucks came, he crept closer, the glow dusting his knees.

A little leaf woman, gold like dollar store holly, clung to her branch as she pulled apart, her glow fading.

"You miss your home," Dakota said, aching for the street light that filled his window.

Dakota scooped the lady up. Once back in the trees, she would glow again, for him, and for everyone at camp.

The lady crumbled into gold dust in his hands, trailing into motes of light.

Dakota stopped. He saw her in his mind, glowing gold…and his tears dried. Why should he share her? They wouldn't understand. He now had something, in his mind, more precious than their cell phones and Nike shoes. Dakota went back to the road, heading for camp. The little gold flicker inside of him had been re-lit. Perhaps if he looked hard enough, one day this summer, he could find another forest companion, and turn that flicker into a flame.

The Staircase Leading Up
Jennifer Bickley

"Sue! Get off! I just fed you an hour ago!" Nikki said, but stroked the grey-striped tabby as he settled onto her lap.

Simon leaned up against the back of Nikki's office chair, currently parked in front of computer, which still had packing peanuts on it "Maybe he's complaining about you spending time in front of that box, instead of putting away those ones." He gestured towards the stacks of cardboard boxes and storage totes that formed a miniature cityscape of towers scattered around their new living room.

The one bedroom apartment, on the second floor of an old, red brick building that smelled of the years of tenants before them had seemed perfect. It was within walking distance of her work and, more importantly, within her and Simon's limited budget.

"I know, I know. I'll get to them," Nikki sighed. "Just let me finish this up first." She turned back towards the screen, trying to ignore her boyfriend as he rested his chin on her shoulder, reading her monitor.

Graphic Design Internship

The Graphic Designer will be an important member of our Team. The primary responsibility of the Graphic Designer will be to create professional quality videos and graphics for print and web.

This is a paid internship. Pay rate based upon performance.

Requirements:

- Student or Recent Graduate in the field of graphic design, digital media arts, multimedia development or related field
- Excellent computer skills and a strong aptitude for learning new

software
- Videography skills an asset.
- Must have at least three years experience in the medical field as a heart surgeon
- Previous experience with website editing an asset.
- Exceptional verbal and written communication skills mandatory
- Must have excellent interpersonal skillss

"Well, they want 'excellent interpersonal skill -ess', Simon pronounced the typo, making her giggle. "That rules you out, Miss Asperger's Poster Child."

"Hey, I worked retail all through university, Asperger's or no Asperger's! If that doesn't prove my 'interpersonal skills', I don't know what does!"

Nikki felt Simon's breath tickle her ear as he sighed. "Why are you looking for jobs now, anyway? We literally just moved in –"

"And we might be moving right back out if I don't get a new job." Nikki said. "Besides, I didn't go to school for four years –"

"How many years?" Even while looking in the other direction, Nikki could see his eyebrows raise.

"Four...alright fine. Five. And a half. The point is –"

"Look, I told you before, don't worry so much. I have my nursing degree now, and I'm sure I won't be stuck in part time at the Old Folks Home forever. I'll have a hospital job before we know it, and you'll have a real job, not just selling toys to brat kids and exasperated parents," Simon replied.

"Must be nice, living back there in the Nineties. So, where'd you park the DeLorean?"

Simon wrapped his arms around Nikki from behind her chair, in that playful, loving way of his that made it impossible for her to be mad at him for long. "It's a classic British Police Box, if you must know. And I'm serious. We're going to be okay. You, me, Sue," Simon scratched the purring pile of puff behind his ears. "Things might be tight for a couple months, but we'll be fine."

Nikki let herself melt into his embrace, as warm as the June sun outside their new windows. She wanted to believe him. She really did.

• • •

A few flakes of early October snow had started to fall as Nikki finished her 20-minute walk home. Another long afternoon/evening shift at The Toybox, preceded by another morning wasted on more job applications that were almost certain to result in another series of rejection emails, maybe a sad little interview, after which they would, of course, take three weeks to reject her as well...

"Nikki, dear. Are you feeling alright?"

"Wha ... oh, sorry Tabitha," Nikki snapped out of her worry at the sound of her land lady's voice.

The older woman, her black hair tastefully "detailed" with streaks of silver in a way Nikki found quite pretty, stood on the front steps of her old, Victorian house, now divided into a 3-unit apartment building, the evening newspaper and a few envelopes tucked under her arm. "Long shift?" she asked with a gentle smile, that for some odd reason, always reminded her of Sue.

"Yeah, not that it's a bad thing. I need all the shifts I can get." Nikki replied.

"Well, you'd better get inside before the snow really starts to come down. The weather report was calling for a blizzard."

"Wow, really? I don't remember there being one this early in the year since I was a kid." Nikki said, and frowned. "I'd better call Simon and let him know – he's working late tonight, and he might have to take a cab home, in case the bus stops running."

"I thought of that, and gave him a call. I hope you don't mind." Tabitha said.

"No, of course not! I mean, you've been so nice to us since moving in ... that was really thoughtful of you."

"He said he'll try to get off work early, but in case he can't, to 'not worry, he'll be fine,'" Tabitha soothed.

"Yeah, that sounds like him." Nikki checked her own mailbox as she reached the front door. Just junk mail, of course, which she threw into the recycling bin right inside the doorway before the stairs leading up to Nikki and Simon's second storey apartment.

"Nikki. Is there anything bothering you?"

"What? No, no. I'm just tired from work, that's all. Standing for 8 hours will do that, not that I want to sound ungrateful or anything ..."

"Of course not, but let me know if I can help you with anything."

"You already have. I mean, you've given me and Simon a place to stay, at a pretty good rent rate, all things considering. What more could we ask of you?" Nikki said as she started to climb the upwards stairs, waving quickly at Tabitha, who was leaning against her own, main floor apartment door. "Anyway, thanks again for giving Simon a call. I really do appreciate it."

The older woman smiled again, that same, catlike grin. "Any time."

• • •

Nikki went inside and shook her head softly at her land lady's kind words. "If only it were that easy, eh Sue? As nice as Tabitha is, I don't think she can help me here." She sighed, and pulled the crumpled bank statement out of her pocket, glanced at it again, and wished she had not. "Well, I got paid today, but between my student loans and bills, there wasn't enough left for groceries... ugh! How am I going to tell Simon?!"

Sue mewed curiously from his spot in a leftover cardboard box left near her desk. Curiously, or was it hungrily? "I guess you want something now, like – almost – everyone else." Nikki noted as she walked down the hallway to get the cat's food out, glancing at the microwave clock over in her tiny galley kitchen as she did so. 9:45 pm, she had got out of work a bit later than usual. Simon was due home at 2:00 am, unless he was able to get out of work early... but then, would they be able to cover rent this month?

"I can't ask Mom and Dad for any more money, or Aunt Janet. She already did so much, letting me stay with her while going to school." Nikki mused as Sue followed, mewing his annoyance. "Okay, okay. I'm getting your food! Learn some patience, cat!" She opened the door to the closet, barely paying attention to the half filled storage totes that were piled from floor to ceiling with extra stuff brought over from Mom's house, before she had moved out west. Reaching for the cat food, she was slightly surprised she did not bang her elbow on the closet wall, like she usually did...

That was because there wasn't a closet wall.

Where the wall should be, instead, the beginnings of a narrow stairway spiraled upwards, around a dark corner. A creepy feeling slid through her – she knew there hadn't been a staircase in the closet before...but, it was an old building, and it was rather hidden...

"Maybe I just didn't see it before?"

The cat just mewed at his cat food bag, but Nikki hardly heard him.

"Sue...? Do you remember a staircase being there, 'cause I sure as hell don't."

Sue rubbed his head against his cat food bag, and mewed again.

"Okay, okay. Creepy stairways that came out of nowhere aren't as important as you being fed." Nikki looked over her shoulder on her way to Sue's bowl, debating what piece of furniture she could shove against the closet door without Simon's help. She poured the catfood rather robotically, spilling over the edges by quite a bit, and held onto the bag, not sure where to put it since the storage closet now seemed out of the question. Finally settling on the kitchen counter, she started looking through the empty kitchen cupboards, trying to distract herself by figuring out what she and Simon could have for dinner that night...unless they wanted macaroni and cheese again...

"Crap. This is how horror movies start, I know it! But I can't just sit here!" Nikki exclaimed, startling Sue. She grabbed the only thing she could think of in her apartment as a weapon – a toy lightsaber that had been given away as a promo at work, turned her cell phone's screen on, and walked over to the storage closet.

. . .

With Sue following at her heels, Nikki made her way up the staircase. Her hand rested on the banister, and, surprisingly enough, she felt the familiar rectangle of a light switch – something most horror movies tended to lack...unless they didn't work, that is. She gave it a flick, and, rather anti-climatically, the light came on without so much as a flicker. Nikki shrugged. "If I'm going to get killed by ghosts or some freak in a hockey mask or whatever, I might as well see it coming," she told an unimpressed Sue.

"What do you think's up here? A murder dungeon, or some creepy room filled with monster- summoning souvenirs...though aren't those usually in basements?" Nikki asked.

Whatever she expected to find, the posh, brightly lit, modern furnished living room she encountered at the top of the stairs certainly wasn't it. Everything was so white! White carpeting, like indoor snow floored a living room full of fancy white leather furniture, with almost futuristic-looking, silver-coloured end tables and a matching coffee table, set up around a shiny new flat screen TV, with what looked like the newest video game console set up in front of it -- certainly a far cry from the discount futon, old tube TV and her 16-bit system adorning her own living room.

"Wow...this place is...nice." Nikki said, as Sue purred from around her ankles. Nikki picked him up, before he could think to leave his own "first impression" on the leather couch. "But, I thought Tabitha said ours was the top floor. The staircase outside our door doesn't go any higher..." Nikki scanned the room, looking for the unit's door. While there was an entrance way – complete with a coat closet, a nice white welcome mat that spelled out "welcome" in cursive writing, and a nice mirror decorated with border of black rose stems set up on the wall nearby, there was no door. Just a blank, white wall where the apartment's door should be, like someone had forgotten to put it in when the building was built.

"Okay..." while Nikki was trying to think of what to say to that, she noticed another glint of white out of the corner of her eye. It was the kitchen – still smaller than it would be in house, but much bigger and nicer than her own galley. Shiny white cabinets and black, what looked like granite countertops contrasted...artfully ...with the stainless steel appliances. But what got Nikki's attention was a note, written on clean, white, but strangely old-looking paper – this wasn't something found in the usual printer – hanging on the refrigerator by a small, silver magnet. It simply said, in the same kind of cursive writing used on the welcome mat "please, help yourself".

    She picked up the note and turned it over. Nothing was written on the other side. "What do you think?" Nikki asked Sue, who was struggling to get out of her arms. She looked around the apartment again. Yes, it was nice, but it looked...showroom nice. It didn't have that lived in feel, the clutter that came when a place was actually occupied, if her own apartment was any indication. And, there didn't seem to be any way into this place, other than the stairway from her storage closet...

    Nikki opened the fridge.

    The inside of the shiny, modern appliance was fully stocked with all kinds of groceries. Bags of milk, loaves of whole wheat bread, a double carton of eggs, a crisper full of fruits and vegetables – even the brand of hard-to-find banana yogurt she loved. . She looked in the freezer, and found bags of frozen veggies, chicken, French fries, perogies – everything that would be on her ideal grocery list. In the cupboards were a jumbo box of Simon's favourite crackers, cookies, instant potatoes, enough tins of soup to last months, boxes of rice (both white and brown) and a pack of real pasta – not a box of macaroni and cheese or a Ramen noodle in sight. Here was real food! Everything she had on her imaginary list before her miniscule paycheque had kicked her in the financial rear end. It was all here!

    Nikki looked at the note again. Please, help yourself.

    It seemed less of a threat, more of a friendly invitation, the more she read it. It was like the labels in Alice in Wonderland, "eat me", "drink me".

    Well, who was she to argue with a literary classic?

. . .

At 4:00 am, Simon came through the door, exhausted, and covered in snow.

"Hey Sue," he greeted his dozing cat, who opened his eyes a tiny sliver from his box by the desk, before shutting them again. "Sorry I'm late, I had to deal with Mr. Bunker again today. Old fart's still convinced Nikki is actually 'Nicolas.'" As he took off his not-expecting-snow, thin fall jacket, it suddenly occurred to him, Nikki was not in her computer chair. She would usually be working on her job applications long into the night – that, or looking up crap online in a tired haze until he came home.

He kicked off his damp shoes, and walked down the hallway the short distance to their bedroom. Sure enough, Nikki was asleep, covers curled around her like a cocoon. He bent down and gave her a kiss on the forehead. "Hey, you're in bed early."

"Mur..." Nikki mumbled. "Shopping."

"Oh?" Simon glanced over at the kitchen. "Oh hey, you got my Betta crackers! Thanks!" He said, noticing the box on the counter, along with quite a few other boxes and cans. "Was the store near your work having a sale or something?"

"Closet..." Nikki sleepily said, and turned over.

"Closet?" Simon asked, then thought better of it. It was too late to get a real answer. He'd ask again in the morning.

. . .

Morning came, but Nikki, as much as she tried, could not think of a way to explain to Simon just where their groceries had come from, especially since when she went to put Sue's cat food bag away in the now, not-as-but-still-kind-of-creepy storage closet, the staircase was gone.

"It's not like I didn't want to tell him", she rationalized to Sue that afternoon while getting ready for work. "It's just...well? Would you believe me if you hadn't seen it?" Sue gave no answer, of course, other than his typical, condescending cat stare.

If that had been the last time Nikki had seen the "magic staircase" and the apartment it led to, Nikki herself would have just wrote it off as a weird, working-too-hard dream, like the "visions" her co-worker Michael had claimed to see after working a 12-hour shift.

The thing was, it happened again.

One time, when Nikki herself had pulled a 12-hour evening shift, with an early morning one the next day, the staircase had appeared again, just as she was thinking of how nice it would be to not have to be awake and ready to go to work again in just 5 hours. That time, she and Sue had found the Apartment's bedroom, with a big, king-sized bed, covered in fluffy white quilts and pillows – she had sunk into it gratefully. When she awoke to a cat's paw gently pushing her cheek and made her way back "downstairs", she checked her microwave clock...to see only a single hour had passed. She checked her computer clocks, the Weather website, her cell phone, everything said the same, even though it felt like she had slept for a day.

Another day, after a disappointing "day off" filled with more futile job applications, Nikki just felt like she needed a bit of a break, just a time to rest, maybe to curl up with a new book, like the one by her favourite author that she had been aching to read, only it was still in hardcover and she simply could not justify spending that much on a book. In the Apartment that time, the very book she had wanted to read was sitting in that fancy living room, right in the middle of the silver coffee table. A slick black tea kettle had also appeared in the kitchen, surrounded by boxes of her favourite book-reading herbal teas.

It seemed every time she really needed something, just when the world was driving her crazy and she needed a break, the stairway was there. It was like the building itself...just knew.

"I just wish I could tell someone, without sounding crazy" Nikki confided to Sue, who looked at her like she was crazy anyway.

• • •

"Hi, I'd like to return this." Nikki stifled a sigh as another Diamond Space Cadet action figure lay on the counter in front of her. The customer, a woman not too much older than Nikki herself smiled sheepishly. "My son had been going on about this figure for months – I thought it would be a perfect birthday present, but after what happened on the show – "

"Do you have your receipt, Ma'am?" Nikki interrupted the story she had heard about 20 times already that day.

"Oh, yes, it's right here in the bag."

Nikki processed the transaction and directed the mother towards the building set aisle, like she asked. Like any good retail employee should.

"At least this one was polite about it." Her manager, Barb, said in a deadpan, from her pile of paperwork, when the customer was out of earshot.

"Yeah," Nikki agreed. "Every so often you get those that realize that no, the toy store clerks don't, in fact, control what goes on in tv shows, like the special secret character ending up being a girl instead of the guy everyone thought she was. Or anything in real life, for that matter."

"Tell that to the jerk in front of me at the gas station this morning." Barb said without looking up.

Nikki nodded. "That happened to me when I was out with Aunt Janet once. I felt bad for the clerk, I mean, it wasn't his fault the gas station across the street had put down their numbers and his hadn't yet. But to hear the asshole in front of us in line, it was like they had personally conspired against him."

"I don't know why you sound surprised," the no-nonsense manager said, and dug her pen into her carbon paper pad in frustration. "After all, we're just retail workers. It's not like we're people or anything. To jerkwad customers, or to the corporations we work for. We're just disposable office supplies, easily replaced by the next pencil to come along."

"Even managers like you?"

"You've been working here for how long now?"

"Four years."

"Then you should know the answer to that, unlike your idiot wrapped in a moron co-worker. Michael! Have you finished dismantling the Diamond Space Cadet display yet!" Barb yelled across the mostly empty store, to where their co-worker was sitting, surrounded by action figures.

"I still don't know why we can't just stick the other 5 Space Cadets in here? Like, reuse it or something." Michael said, in his usual whiny way.

"Because Head Office emailed and wants the whole thing taken down. 'Girl action figures don't sell', you know." Barb said, still filling out her paperwork.

"That's such bullshit. What's wrong with girl action figures? They're all basically dolls anyway." Nikki complained, looking down at the little silvery white figure in its plastic bubble, that some little boy's mom simply assumed he would not like, just because the character was a girl.

She had completely forgotten the mother was still in the store. And she had just come up the counter, building block set in hand. She didn't say anything, but glared daggers at Nikki as Barb got up from her paperwork and did the sale.

After the customer finally left, Barb turned to her. "What have I told you about paying attention to customers in the store?"

"To pay attention, and not say anything 'opinionated' around them." Nikki mumbled to her feet.

"You've been doing so well lately too. What's wrong?" Barb said. She genuinely sounded concerned.

"It's just, the job search still hasn't been going well...but that's no excuse. I'm sorry."

Barb sighed. "Be careful what you say. Remember, we're just sales people, not people people, at least not while here. Now, go help Michael with the Space Cadets. And put the Amber, Pearl, and now Diamond ones in the back rows. Upsell the boys, or the DM will be pissed if he comes in here, no matter how messed up that seems to you."

"Yeah, the girl ones have cooties!" Michael added.

"Enough from the peanut gallery, or I'll make you arrange the pink aisle by shade!" Barb retorted. "You sure you're okay, Nikki?"

"Yeah, it's just...have you ever wished you could tell people about something, but they'd think you were crazy if you opened your mouth?"

Barb then looked at Nikki like she was crazy, or at least,

crazier than usual. "You do know we work retail, right?"

"Yeah. Good point."

• • •

"Hey, Nikki! Had the afternoon shift today?"

"Oh, hey Maria." Nikki greeted her downstairs neighbour Maria, who worked at the bank nearby, and her little two-year old daughter, Paige, who waved hello from her stroller.

"Need a walking-home buddy today?"

"Oh, sure! That would be nice." Nikki answered, a little nervously. Still, she remembered Simon's advice on 'small talk'. "So, how are you doing?" she asked, while turning onto the sidewalk.

"Well, it could be better. Josh still hasn't found another job since the factory closed..."

Nikki usually found it difficult to talk to people, but luckily, it seemed Maria just needed someone to vent to, and, well, she could relate. She listened as Maria described the troubles her husband Josh had been having. They had just started trying for Paige, when his factory had shut down, and he had been out of work since then, not for a lack of trying. Maria herself was barely supporting her family on her bank teller's job, even with full time hours and above minimum wage.

Nikki listened to her frustration, her worry, with a sense of familiarity, but with more urgency. It was bad enough when this kind of thing happened to Simon and her, but for a family with a growing baby...

"Maria," she interrupted. "If I tell you something that sounds absolutely crazy, but I just know will help you, will you believe me?"

"Nikki? What are you talking about? Are you okay?" Maria said.

"It's about our building..." Nikki began, as she stopped at the stop sign at the last intersection before their building. Maria waved, and Nikki looked over – Tabitha was on the steps again, this time watering the new spring flower beds adjacent to them. She waved back, but then, her wave turned into a sudden, upwards motion of her arms.

Maria screamed, and, as if in a bullet time movie, Nikki saw the SUV bending the stop sign right beside them.

But the vehicle was frozen, the stop sign just starting to buckle under its weight, the driver also frozen in time, a cell phone up to his ear, yet to notice he had driven up on the curb.

"Run across, now! I can't hold him forever!" Tabitha yelled, her arms still thrown upwards, as if she were pushing something...

Too shocked to question, Nikki pulled Maria and the baby across the road, safely home.

. . .

"I know you have questions. I would too."

Once again, Nikki sat in the Apartment, on the white leather couch, a warm cup of peppermint tea in her hands, though for once, she had more than just Sue for company. Maria sat in the recliner, holding Paige to her, tears still streaming down her face. Tabitha came out from the kitchen, and gave her a matching cup of tea to what Nikki held, a soft, but still catlike smile on her face.

"I do, and I'm sure Maria does too. I think we're just trying to figure out where to start." Nikki began.

"Well, that's as good a place as any, I suppose." Tabitha replied. "As you might have guessed, this isn't a normal apartment. This place is a place that I made, in order to help those who need it."

"Just...what are you?" Maria asked.

Tabitha looked distant for a few minutes, then began her answer. "We're called by many names. We were once called gods, then fae, the fair folk, spirits, or even angels. But basically, when humans feel strongly enough about an idea, a certain concept or thought, we manifest."

"That doesn't explain just how you saved our lives back there, not that I'm ungrateful or anything." Maria said, and hugged little Paige closer, who complained "no, Mommy" and pushed her mother back a little, more interested in the picture book Tabitha had given her than whatever the adults were talking about.

"I don't really know how I did it myself. I just knew I had to do something, so I did it, and it was done."

"That doesn't make any sense." Maria said.

"Does the world you live in make any more sense? A world where people like the two of you can work hard, get an education, do everything 'right', and still be treated the way you are? Barely surviving in an unfair system. I don't like that." Tabitha pursed her lips. "I don't like that at all. And I want to do something, no, I need to do something about it. So, I bought this house. And I paid good, honest workers to divide it into apartments. Then, I made this place, this...'prototype', I guess you could call it. I'm still working on making it comfortable."

"I think you're doing a pretty good job so far," Nikki began, "but to be honest, though it does seem a little..."

"Showroom-y". Maria nodded. "I thought so the first time the stairway showed up for me as well."

Nikki opened her mouth to say something, then closed it. Of course it would be there for Maria.

"Hey, this place kept me stocked in diapers for months!" Maria added, seeing the look on Nikki's face.

"Ah, I thought so, but I wasn't sure about that." Tabitha nodded, taking the "constructive criticism" in stride. "Anyway, I want to eventually have more buildings, help more people with this Place, just as it has helped you."

"But...why do you want to help so much?" Nikki had to ask. "I mean, I don't want to sound ungrateful or anything but..."

"Don't worry, you don't." Tabitha looked out the window, towards the sunny spring day as sunlight shined through it, through her, her grey highlights shimmering. "That world out there, it could be so much more beautiful, if only Greed would release its grip. If only more people felt the feeling that Created me, so long ago..."

"Tabitha?"

"Oh, I'm sorry. Anyway, I'm sorry I can't help with everything. I can't find your families' the positions you need, that you deserve, but I can help you, and anyone else that needs it, while they help themselves, as long as they never lose hope. All I ask is if you're ever in a position to do the same, you do so."

• • •

"Nikki, where do you want these...ah!" The intern almost fell from the stack of printer paper he was carrying.

"Stephen, are you okay?" Nikki asked.

"Yeah, it's just...I got a summer job over at the Toy Box, but the university's going to kick me out of Residence at the end of the term. I need a place to stay, but sorry, I shouldn't let that bother me at work."

"Hey, just be glad there are graphic design internships for students now. There weren't when I was your age." Nikki turned in her desk chair, almost knocking down her family picture of her, Simon, and their two young children, taken outside "Aunt Tabitha's" apartment building.

Nikki propped up the picture, and smiled as she turned back to her intern. "You know what, Stephen? I just might know someone who can help you."

No Good Deed Goes Unpunished
Tecuma Macintyre

On Sunday nights, East Harbor was dead. Stores in the shopping complex closed around seven o'clock, while the restaurants would remain open for another two hours. Save for the occasional drunken tourist and the security guard patrols, the covered walkways were empty. At the southernmost tip of the shopping plaza, a bookstore was locked up, colorful shutters pulled tightly against the windows and doors. Inside it, the only illumination came from a flashlight and several hurricane lanterns set up in strategic locations. A table had been pulled into the middle of the store, a honey-blond haired woman, Abby, removing items from a backpack and placing them on the surface. Next to her, a short-haired black woman, Michelle, watched the proceedings, a worried look on her face. Both were wearing jeans and t-shirts, though the blond wore a leather thong necklace with a moonstone resting in the hollow of her throat.

"Are you certain this is going to work?" She asked, folding her arms across her chest. "I mean-Abby, I can't afford any more bad luck. Not now. Not when the store's finally starting to see the black, and I just got the landlords to agree to another year's lease..."

"It's going to work." Abby said soothingly, protecting an aura of calmness in her voice. "By this time tomorrow, everything's going to be normal in here again, and the only problems you're going to have to deal with are your normal ones, like the bratty teenagers from the local high school or the grumpy rich old farts from the island." At this a smile twitched on Michelle's face, her muscles relaxing slightly.

"Listen to you, talking like a native. Now all you truly need to do to fit in is attend temple like so many of us around here," she said.

Abby grinned at that as she started to pour a bottle of water into a bowl, her green eyes gleaming with mischief as she glanced over.

"Michelle, if I took one step inside a synagogue everything might catch fire. Not to mention your mother's friends might suspect you of starting to play for the other team." She said teasingly. Michelle scowled, squaring her shoulders.

"I'm in no rush for another relationship. Not now. It's too soon, Peter…" She trailed off, suddenly swiping at her eyes. "God. It's just been such a rotten year. First my father, then Peter and that - that floozy, the IRS, and the hurricanes…" Her voice cracked. "I haven't been able to have just a moment to breathe, and when I finally get one-" Abby stopped what she was doing and moved to wrap her arms around her friend.

"Hey, hey." Michelle looked up at her, sniffling. "I said it'd be alright, wouldn't I? I just wish you'd contacted me sooner." The black haired woman drew in a breath to compose herself, running the back of her hand over her eyes.

"I wanted to, but it didn't feel right. You've only been down here a few months, and I didn't know if you'd recovered your own bearings." She withdrew out of the hug, picking up a flashlight from the table and fiddling with it. "Not to mention…well…" She risked a nervous glance up at the interior of the bookstore. "This is embarrassing." Abby had returned to her preparations. She looked up from wrapping a rosary around her left wrist.

"I'm sorry?" Michelle had the grace to flush, but she continued with her train of thought.

"It's embarrassing. Like one of those cheesy paranormal shows that are so popular right now. This sort of thing just doesn't happen in this area. And no offense to you, but if any of my customers or the other store owners around here found out what I was doing, I'd probably be a laughingstock." She said. "I - I mean, I don't even know how this happened."

"Various theories abound on that, but I've got a fairly good inclination of what happened." Abby responded, setting down a bundle of herbs and picking up a small black-handled dagger. "But I won't be able to confirm it until after I've done the banishing, so here." Michelle jumped as a hand briskly pulled at a sleeve to move her away from the table. "Stand here for a moment, and hold this."

A small wooden disk with a pentacle carved on it was placed into a hand.

"W-wait what? What am I doing?"

"I need you out of harm's way while I'm performing the ritual." Abby said. *Not to mention that your fears could bleed over into mine, and if that happens we can forget about saving the bookstore.* "Keep the carved side face out, and just think happy thoughts while you're in the circle."

"Happy thoughts?" Michelle repeated dumbly. "What does that do?"

"It keeps you from worrying. If you don't worry, the spirit won't be looking at you as a source of energy, and it'll make it weaker." *Instead it's going to be looking at me, with all the nervous energy I've got. Ever since I've agreed to this, I could run the entire power grid for the east coast of Florida.* Drawing in a deep breath, Abby let her third eye open, channeling power down her arm and though the hilt of the knife, gathering in the blade. She began to move clockwise around Michelle, enclosing her friend in a protective circle of energy. If done correctly, the combination of the shield and pentacle would keep the other woman safe from harm. A year ago, she wouldn't have needed to add a pentacle - or use an athame. She'd been at the point where she could cast magic without the ritual instruments, a simple wave of her hands and her will ensured exactly what she wished done...

One impulsive European tour later - ending with a nightmare in Austria - and she was the shell of the witch she used to be. Face betraying no emotion, Abby returned to the table - picking up a box of matches to light the herbal bundle. Flames flickered for a moment, and then settled into embers as the smell of sage and sweetgrass started to fill the air. Almost immediately there was a reaction - Abby's eyes caught a shadow flicking from bookshelf to bookshelf, and she couldn't help the involuntary tensing of her muscles.

It's okay. You can do this. You can do this. Squaring her shoulders, Abby left the relative safety of the table and walked over to the store's front doors, holding both of her hands high in the air. "In the name of Jesus, Mary Magdalene, and Archangel Michael, I banish all negative forces from this space. Let it be filled with light and love." She started to gently wave the herb bundle, letting smoke drift about. "Let this space be a harbor of peace for both mind and body." With that, she began to walk the perimeter of the store, waving the smoke onto bookshelves, furniture, any and all openings that were present in her line of sight. "To any negative spirits in this place, you are not welcome. If you are not sent from God, you are not welcome." Her voice quivered slightly, and Abby quickly swallowed, risking a glance back at Michelle. Her friend seemed fine, shining the flashlight on the areas that had been smudged.

Please, please. Let this go well. Let what happened in Austria have stayed in Austria. Michelle didn't know this, but this was the first major spell working Abby had dared try in a year. Paralyzing fear of what she'd encountered - a coven gone mad, secrets about her family - and relatives that just outright *refused* to stay dead - it had been too much for her to handle. The nervous breakdown had been a small blessing, but with her mind in recovery she'd been unable to summon even the most basic shields - to keep anything from latching onto her and following. When she'd made it back to the United States Abby had limited herself to solitary practice, working only 'small magics' such as ones for luck and health. It was a rule of thumb in her world that the larger the magic was, the more it would attract things of any intent. She had intended to never again do any larger spells…but a tearful phone call from Michelle had eroded her resolve.

She's had so much trouble lately. What good am I as a witch if I can't even help my friends? Abby was moving on automatic as she kept walking through the store, waving the sage and sweetgrass. *Or is it that my willpower just sucks when it comes to my-* Out of the corner of her left eye she saw a shadow lunge at her. On impulse Abby spun around, thrusting out the herbal bundle. The shadow recoiled in upon itself, scuttling back to a bookshelf and trying to squeeze itself in between the paperbacks. Glancing upward, Abby noticed that she was in the New Age section - and if she looked behind her, she'd covered nearly all of the store save for this particular zone. The entity was beginning to hiss and spit, it seemed as if she'd cornered it in its place of origin.

"Bingo." Michelle seemed to go on high alert at that, beaming the flashlight at the bookshelves.

"You found it?"

"Uh-huh." Bracing herself - both physically and mentally - Abby advanced on the shadow, keeping her hands out in front of her. In her ears she could hear a low hissing noise, and her third eye was twitching wildly. An oppressive feeling lurked just beyond the boundary of her energy shield-making itself known with a heavy pressure against her skin. The more she moved forward, the harder it was becoming to simply just walk-it was if she was moving through mud. The entity haunting the bookstore knew she wanted it gone and was using every trick in its book to repel her.

Lucky for me it doesn't have a lot of tricks. This particular creature was ridiculously low on the totem pole for paranormal beings, a novice-level energy creation. When the paranormal activity first started, it had been relatively small - customers and employees had reported becoming angry for no good reason, people had seen shadows dart about and a few books had gone flying off shelves. Things had become serious after a child had been scratched during a story time in the kids' department, and Michelle herself had been attacked psychically in her office. That had resulted in the hysterical phone call that had brought Abby to her friend's aid - Michelle had sounded as if she was on the verge of a nervous breakdown. Fearing for her sanity, Abby had agreed to come and banish whatever was haunting the bookstore. Shaking her head to keep herself focused and in the present, Abby stepped forward, steeling herself for any retaliation.

"Saint Michael the Archangel, defend us in battle, be our protection against the malice and snares of the devil-" the hissing turned into screeching. In the protective circle, Michelle bit back a scream as a blob of grayish-black energy hurled itself at Abby, slamming into an invisible barrier a foot away from her. The divine energy from the prayer's spoken words was beginning to hurt it, the blob twisting and writhing in mid-air. "I humbly beseech you oh God to command him, and do you, O Prince of the heavenly host-" The rosary began to glow with a golden light as one tendril slammed against that invisible wall, trying to grab at the witch's outstretched hands. The pressure had now turned into a full-blown migraine, and Abby gritted her teeth, focusing her attention on the prayer. "by the divine power, cast into hell Satan and all those evil spirits who roam this world seeking the destruction of souls!" Another screech of pain, and the blob recoiled in upon itself, falling to the ground. The feeling of heaviness in her legs began to recede - as did the headache, and Abby bent over to wave the herbal bundle and the rosary over the creature.

"In the name of Jesus the God, and Mary Magdalene the Goddess, I banish you from this place!" She chanted, feeling power surge up and down her arms. "In the name of Archangel Michael, general of the armies of heaven, I bless this space and make it holy!" In her field of vision, golden energy was wrapping itself around the gray-black blob, forcing it to contract and vaporize. "As I will this, so mote it be!" With a low cry the creature gave up the struggle and vanished-leaving behind a red paperback book. The store was silent for several moments, and then Michelle spoke, her voice quivering.

"Is it over?"

"It is." Abby replied, glancing around. On the magical plane everything else was also silent - the sage and sweetgrass smoke settling into the area, creating barriers against harmful energies. And thankfully...not a hint of anything else - energy creature or vengeful spirit. Abby let out a breath she hadn't realized she'd been holding, tension seeping out of her muscles.

Oh thank you. Thank you, thank you, thank you. She still had her magic, she still could call upon her spirits and deities...
A flare of energy had her turning around - Michelle was about to step out of the protective circle. "Hold it! Don't move - I need to release you from that!" The other woman froze, and Abby hurried over, stopping at the table along the way to drop the herbal bundle into the bowl of water and pick up her athame. Cutting a line in the circle, she moved counterclockwise to gather up the energy as Michelle hurried over to where the creature had been, bending over to pick up the book.

"Hexing and the Art of Black Magick." She read loud. "That thing came from this?"

"Open it up." Her friend instructed. A puzzled look crossed Michelle's face, but she obeyed. An index card slipped out from the book's pages, falling to the ground. The bookstore owner moved back, picking up the card and beginning to read it. Her brows furrowed.

"This is about…somebody named Cindy, and she's upset because her friend Janet stole her boyfriend Robbie. So this is her intent - hey!" Abby had come back over, nipping the card from Michelle's fingers.

"Basically, some brokenhearted twit teenager came into your store, pulled this book from your New Age section, and cast one of the spells in here. Only she didn't do it right, and what she summoned decided to stay in the store and feed off the negative energy of anything that came in here." She said. "More than likely it decided to stay because there was leftover negative energy from everything that's happened to the store over the past year. This place definitely needed a cleansing." Her fingers deftly bagged the index card. Michelle bit her lower lip, a worry coming to the forefront of her mind.

"Nothing else is going to come in here now, is it?" She ventured, looking at Abby. The blond woman sighed gustily, shoulders sagging.

"You can't prevent negative energy from ever entering a place. That will happen. And considering somebody worked magic here - magical workings do attract things both good and bad. You probably more than likely are going to have to cleanse your store - smudging it, like I did tonight - every so often." She began. "And for the love of everything - if there's teenagers in your New Age section, or anyone who looks as if they might try something from one of the books you have, stop them. They may have latent magical talent enough to manifest something like what we dealt with tonight, or may be doing it on purpose." Michelle slowly nodded, not looking very happy. Abby forced a smile onto her face, reaching out to touch her friend on the shoulder.

"I'll come by tomorrow morning and double-check the place while it's open. But as of now, you don't need to worry; you have your store back." The black haired woman nodded, a faint smile crossing her lips at that statement.

• • •

Morning had turned into afternoon by the time Abby made it back to the Bookworm. The store was busy - customers being rung out and leaving with purchases, employees filling orders - and the air felt much lighter and cheerful. Michelle was entertaining children with a puppet show, and every so often there was a burst of laughter. Abby stuck her hands in her pockets and watched as her friend worked - Michelle looked much healthier, a glow suffusing her skin, her aura bright and clean.

"Please let it all be over for her." She murmured silently. "Grant her good fortune." As if in response a warm feeling passed Abby by on her right side, causing her to turn her head. The ghostly image of an elderly man dressed in church clothes and wearing a yarmulke offered a wave, and the woman blinked in surprise. It was Charles Yeskal - Michelle's father. The spirit gave Abby a mischievous wink, and then moved to sit down next to his daughter. Unable to help it, a broad smile broke across Abby's face; here was a fitting answer to her prayers. Even in the afterlife, Charles still wanted to care for both his daughter and the bookstore. If he was still strong in spirit, in death as he had been in life, Michelle wouldn't need to worry about any negative paranormal activity. If her father felt the urge to play a few pranks every now and again though… Biting her lips to keep a giggle from breaking free, Abby turned around and decided to head over to the New Age shelves to see if there were any new books in stock.

She began to walk forward…and then stopped in her tracks, muscles tensing. Her third eye opened - magical senses flaring to life, everything around her seemed to be slowing down - muting itself. The people around her, their conversations…even time itself was now a trickle. The feeling of something pressing against her was back, but Abby couldn't sense any intent in it. What she could pick up was a nothingness, which was a stark contrast compared to the bustle of life that was around her. Curious, Abby began to turn around, but stopped as just out of the corner of her right eye, she saw a cream-colored wing and a flash of copper light.

Take warning. Once you see it, you go down a path from which there is no turning back. A male voice echoed in her thoughts. In the back of her mind, Abby recognized the voice as the angel Gabriel's own, but curiosity had her completing the turn before rational thought could intercede. Her gaze fell on one of the large windows at the Bookworm's front, and a scream bubbled up in her throat. Standing in front of the window was a black-haired woman, her dusty skin betraying Middle-Eastern ancestry. She was petite, wearing a pair of blue jeans and a red sweater. Her hair hung about her face in wet clumps, green eyes fixed on Abby's terrified blue ones. In the haze of shock, Abby felt her mouth opening, her tongue speaking a name that she'd tried so hard to forget over the past year.

"D-D-Devyani?" She stammered out. Now named, the spirit nodded. Raising her right hand she gestured, indicating that Abby should come out. Numbly, the blond woman shook her head no, a part of her mind noticing that the store's cleansing was keeping the spirit out. That meant one of two things - either she was about to have a very public encounter with an angry ghost, or that the newly-created barriers were too strong for Devyani to breach. Devyani's eyes narrowed and she turned her right hand so that the palm was facing outward. Abby's eyes flicked to it, and she sucked in sharp breath as she recognized what was on the skin. Imprinted on the flesh in black ink was a stylized sun-with a small pentagram inside it.

Oh no. She didn't, she didn't. Fear was starting to sink its claws into her, the darkness she thought she'd been able to banish looming on the edge of her mind. Hearing her breath come out in small pants as adrenaline began to flood her body - the telltale signs of a panic attack - Abby started to move backwards, shaking her head.

"No. No! If you got yourself involved with them, it's on you! It's on you! Not me!" Devyani's lips seemed to curl into a snarl, and the features of her face began to change. The nails on her hands began to grow out and curl, inky blackness replacing the green irises of her eyes. Her face became hollow, the flesh starting to rot away over her cheekbones as the clothes on her body began to rot. Dimly Abby could feel an upsurge of power - Charles had detected something was wrong and was reacting. A white-gold creature lurched out from one of the bookshelves - the Jewish section? - and barreled towards the front window, passing though it and hurling itself on top of Devyani. A muted scream had Abby slapping her hands over her ears as the spirit vanished. Charles' creature - a golem? - pulled itself up from off the ground, lumbering back into the store and vanishing into the bookshelf it had come from. With Devyani's disappearance time resumed its normal flow, and Abby was left panting and crying silently in the middle of the store. Customers stopped to look at her, and Michelle looked up from her puppet play. Seeing the distraught woman, she quickly handed over the strings to another employee and rushed over.

"Abby? Abby? Oh dear God - Joseph, help me here!" Strong hands took her by the shoulders, and started to lead her towards the back. "Somebody go get me a cold cloth. Here Abby, you just need to sit down-"

"No!" With a cry Abby twisted herself free, backing away. Michelle and her employee stared at her. Abby was certain she looked as if she'd lost her mind. *Not again, not again. Please, not again.*

"Abby please, just come in the back, sit down and catch yourself…" Michelle reached out, taking her friend by the wrist. Then she jerked in shock as Abby yanked herself free.

"I said no! Leave me alone!" Not stopping to see the look of hurt that crossed the other woman's face - or Charles's outstretched hand - Abby turned and ran out of the store, hot tears blinding her. The only clear thought in her mind was to get distance - to run, run away as fast as she could right now. If she ran, she could make it back to her house, where it was safe - where she could pray, gather her thoughts…and begin to pack.

The Home Tree
Elizabeth McLean

The following excerpt was found on Maureen Tullio's hard drive in the weeks following her death. It appears to be a redacted piece of her 2032 autobiography, An Emotional Mosaic. We included it in this anthology to provide a more accurate picture of the inner life of the author and her private struggles with what appear to be intermittent hallucinations.

-*The Editors*

And certainly, in order for me to view my subjects with the depth and dignity that all human beings (and many animals) possess, I had to learn many lessons, each that brought me closer to our shared humanity. Ironically enough, the first and foremost powerful lesson in compassion that I learned was not, strictly speaking, taught to me by someone whom I believe to be totally human.

It was the early twenty-tens, and I had just clawed my way up through internship hell (for more on that see Chapter 3) into a more-or-less steady job writing for the Drakeford Gazette.

For those of you who don't know Drakeford, it's a mid-sized town which is conveniently sandwiched in the corridor between Hamilton and Toronto, close enough to attract Torontonians looking for a more laid-back lifestyle, and just far enough away to be off the beaten trail. Like many such towns, it never really grows or shrinks much, but perpetually harbors ambitions of becoming a Mississauga or a Burlington, someplace with three shopping malls and a movie theatre with in-show meals delivered to your seat.

When I arrived in Drakeford, the election had just passed, and the new mayor was a determined sort with an eye to provincial level politics, and so, naturally, next came the resurrection of the big Drakeford Supermall project. The original project had been scrapped some five years earlier due to the developers' realization that Southern Ontario needed another giant mall like Disneyland needed more Mickey, and some rather fervent environmental protests on behalf of an ancient, endangered cottonwood tree growing in the middle of the site. Times being what they were, nobody really considered the protesters a factor in the mall's demise. The corporation, far from being scared off by their sit-ins and pamphlets, just kind of got bored and wandered away, to the benefit of all concerned.

This was the backdrop under which my friend and colleague, Robert Ling, wandered into my cubicle one slow summer news day as I was finishing an article about a local pet store's disappearing goldfish problem. (Footnote: In retrospect, the store in question kept an awful lot of free-range rescue cats.)

"Maureen!" he said to me, arms outstretched, "I've just assigned you your first big story. How would you like to write a feature on the big Supermall controversy?"

My heart thrilled. I smiled my biggest smile, with all the innocence a green twenty-two year old can muster.

" I get to talk to the mayor? I get to outline the debate? Bob, this is fantastic! I could change the course of the whole town!"

Bob looked uncomfortable. Nothing good ever came of him scratching his right arm like that.

"Not exactly, he said, "Jeremy's going to handle the big debate piece on the Monday. It's going to be a series, where we break it down issue by issue. You've got Laurel Bolton."

"Laurel Bolton?" I said at the time, "They played her out on the last attempt at the Supermall. Weeks and weeks of coverage of her sitting there, chained to a tree."

They had, too. The coverage had been hackneyed when they started, and by the end everyone in town agreed the horse was dead, and the bones had been whipped to dust. The woman gave one good interview, and then all she did was repeat herself. And now I was going to be repeating myself, all over a feature everyone would groan at. I had been begging for a feature, a real human interest story (or hell, even one of those sensationalist ones about how fat people fail at life or feminism is outdated would have had the desired effect at the time). But this...

"This is impossible for me to do well, Bob. It's played out. Laurel Bolton is irrelevant."

Bob sighed, and gave me a look, mouth turned down, forehead wrinkled, that I would in later years come to associate with him being forced to abandon foreign correspondents in the field.

"Well, Maureen, if you can't make this one work, you won't get another. I suggest you use your imagination. I know you have one. I've peeked in your notebooks at lunch. Very sexy stuff, by the way. Do this well, and next year you could be up with Jeremy. Think of that when you want to complain."

Jeremy was a bit of a prig, and I hold that no one would actually want to share office space with him if given the choice. But I did want his job, and so that night, after the missing goldfish had been thoroughly memorialized, I stayed at work, scanning through the archives from the last Supermall series. I found thirty articles, all on Laurel Bolton and her group, covering everything from their home lives to their personal philosophies... even an article sharing their favourite vegan recipes. Every angle I could think of had been taken.

At least, every decent, honourable angle had been taken. The only lack I could find after endless searching was a lack of dirt. You would think environmentalists would have plenty of that.

So, with the construction date, and my deadline, looming, I determined to stick to the protesters like glue, and exploit any small hypocrisy or weakness. Nobody really cares what they say or do anyway, I thought. Barring a major explosion or a spontaneous oil spill at the developers' headquarters, the mall would go up, and no amount of coverage either way would make a difference. It all came down to he said, she said, they said, etc and the general public was so bored of the facts by now that they'd do anything to avoid more discussion of the matter. The only person this series might benefit is me, I thought, so why not play whatever angle I can?

Still, as I entered the chilly spring night, heading home, I shivered harder than usual, racked with guilt and nervous anticipation. But then, I remembered all the freezing nights I'd spent during internships, low on food, low on blankets, low on everything but dreams. And I'd been one of the lucky ten percent of my class that had even scored an internship. My heart hardened. No, I wasn't ever letting myself go back there, to that place of crying on grocery days and explaining to relatives that I wasn't unemployed but I also didn't make money and getting that look that said 'I could have done better in your shoes.' They'd called me off the bench in a game with skewed rules, but I was going to play, and if I had to play dirty, so be it.

Early the next day, so tired that I tripped over my own feet on the way from the bus, I reached the as-yet-empty lot where the protesters gathered around the old cottonwood tree. I had donned my most approachable, granola-coated professional gear: a multi-layered dark green maxi skirt, a folksy pinstriped dress top, and a wood-inlay bead necklace. I wore my old college backpack, rather than the shiny high-end purse I used on work days.

As I traipsed across the field, careful to avoid the copious brambles, I grew a large, hopefully disarming grin. The cottonwood stood there, waiting for me, a dark guardian with twisted limbs, a tall, proud trunk, and layers of cracked and broken bark that twisted up and around its sides. Even in the harsh light of morning turning into afternoon, its whole being emitted shade, cool, and still of night. In this shade, a small ring of men and women that one might find on college campuses everywhere holding up signs about the evils of shampoo knelt on cushions around one remarkable woman.

Although she looked thinner than the chains binding her to the tree, and her skin was so moon-pale that I longed to drag her out from the shade into the sun, Laurel Bolton drew her strength from the earth. Nestled in between the cottonwood's roots, she took on the aspect of something rooted to the land she grew up on. When she looked at me, her striking blue eyes betrayed no uncertainty. She caught me unawares even at that early moment, and standing there, the two of us assessing one another, I learned simultaneously the sheer power and utter hopelessness of using a dead photo to capture the essence of another living being. What had looked drab and homely on paper, now looked rooted and radiant.

I fumbled for my notes. This woman could well prove fascinating, if only I could ask the right questions, but all I could think of, and all that I had on my notepad, were variations on the questions that others had asked before me. And honestly... how did one interview for the sublime?

So, I sat down with her, and asked her my questions, praying for some stroke of fate to bring me the answer that would reveal her to my readers.

"Why have you decided to come and protest the mall again, with rumours circulating that your health is in decline?"

"This is my home. I have to defend it the best I know how."

"What made you decide to fight for this particular cause?"

"The Trees are my family. We all share the earth, and I am part of the balance of life here."

"Why don't you take more dramatic steps to get out into the world and make yourself known?"

"I have a daughter. I would never do anything to put her in danger."

Scanned articles scrolled through my head. A thousand interviews, at a thousand different times, and I could have plugged those answers into any one of them. I excused myself for lunch, secretly seething.

Back on the heat of the tarmac, someone emerged from a black car that I hadn't registered on the way in. He was skinny, around my age, and sporting a scraggly mustache and sort-of beard. He also wore the uniform of a local security company. The mall had hired him to keep an eye on the protesters, he said, and to make sure everything stayed calm. I asked him if he'd seen anything strange in the past week or so, since things started up again.

For a moment, he scowled at me, and I wondered if his intentions were entirely honourable.

"There's been something happening at night, and my boss said to save it for the news. You look like the news," he said to me, motioning me toward the E-Z Mart across the street.

For a moment I hesitated when he wanted to take me into the back room of the little bodega, whose floors had a patina of scuff marks thirty years old and whose air smelled like rotten lettuce and old cold cuts. When I saw the security television in the corner, I eased up a bit.

"We paid the owner to use one of his security cameras. We've had it locked on Bolton 24/7," he said. He thrust a DVD into the system, and selected the footage from a couple of nights previous.

"Get a load of this," he said, with a smirk that told me that showing girls grainy security footage was the closest he ever got to getting laid. He pointed at the time code. On screen, Laurel Bolton lay under the tree, arms folded, sleeping.

"Five minute delay," he said, "Now you see her..."

The footage refreshed, and the chains were there, but, no Laurel.

"Poof," he said, "Make of it what you will. My bosses just wanted you to know all the facts."

I thanked him for his time and left the bodega, a sandwich in one hand and my voice recorder in the other. I had a sleeping bag stored in the garage at my parents' place, and I was going to need it.

As the sun set over the fields, and the crickets began their choral work, I reflected to myself that my day had been punctuated by trudging through itchy grass and weeds. I had changed out of my hippie gear earlier in the day, in favour of black skinny jeans and a comfy pullover, but still the grass somehow managed to itch and poke at me through the denim. Early on, I tripped over a stick lodged in a dried-up mud pit. I looked back, hoping that Bob had already left, but of course, he was still there, watching. He gave me a thumbs-up. I think my face lit up hot enough to burn off my eyebrows. At least I hadn't dropped the camera.

When I reached my destination, a section of ruined barn wall jutting up out of the ground that would both provide cover and a good angle for viewing Bolton in secret, I heard Bob get back into his car, shut the door and drive away. Minutes after spreading my sleeping bag and settling in, I was mightily glad I had brought insect repellent. The area around the ancient wooden pillars felt damp and sticky, and mosquitoes whined in my ears, causing me to slap myself upside the head several times before learning to ignore it. I had gone to this much trouble to avoid notice; there was no sense blowing my cover with a ton of movement, bugs or no bugs.

With Bob's help, I had chosen a spot that allowed me to see Laurel clearly, from the side, but that also allowed me to sneak in from the back of the field without being seen. As the last pink of the sunset drained from the sky, I hunkered down, camera at the ready, peeking through a gap in the old boards and breathing in their cold, musty aroma. Laurel, her brothers and sisters in arms gone for the night, dozed beneath a homely old patchwork blanket, still and serene. The moon, and the distant streetlamps illuminated her with a mild, yellow-white rim light.

As I waited there, growing stiff with the passing minutes and hours, growing itchy with the caresses of stiff grass and bug bites, still the light of the moon, and the sound of the crickets, and the whole quiet power of the place, and the dark, and the stars, slowly filled me with a sense of anticipation and wonder, like a cup slowly filling under a trickling spring. The cottonwood tree stretched to enormous proportions, brushing the sky, finally fully in its element. I found myself looking up, in spite of myself, wondering at the dome of the heavens. I had slept under the Sky Dome once, on a school trip, and I remember looking up and feeling dwarfed by how vast the roof of the stadium really was, with its tiny seats stretching down toward us. How much more vast was this construction of the sky, forged by an architect that none of us could fathom, but to whom we all owed the very core of our being?

After one such foray into the sky, I came back to Laurel, and found her changed. She had twisted around to caress the tree, her pale, pointed little face facing up into the branches with a look of love and devotion consuming her features. She lay her head on the tree's trunk, paper skin to rough, cracked bark, and at that moment, I felt the affinity between them, the delicate little woman of the day and the tall, strong tree of the night. Seeing them then, I could not deny that they were two aspects of the same creature.

As she touched the trunk, Laurel's hand melted into the bark, becoming a strange, twisted set of branches, like a shrub that has grown into a section of frost fence. I closed my eyes hard and re-opened them, even going so far as to prick myself on the end of a nearby stick, but no matter what I did, when I looked back at Laurel, she still melted slowly into the bark of the tree, like a chunk of ice melting into a puddle. Half of her body entered the tree, and then, her face, which had up until this point been pressed against the trunk, melted and changed as well, her skull flattening into bark, her eyes disappearing into knot hollows... but before they melted away entirely, I could see, no, feel that the last thing her eyes focused on was me.

Soon she was gone, and all that remained was the tree, dark and silent, silhouetted against the night. I felt a peace ripple over the field, permeating the very ground. For a moment, I felt rooted to the spot, invisible tubers flowing out of my fingertips and toes where they met the ground.

The tree swayed in an unfelt breeze, no, turned to me, and despite its lack of eyes, I could feel the gaze of something ancient, something that smelled like ages of decaying leaves and sweet running sap, opening itself to me, allowing me to see into its core. My heart filled with the cool of a thousand summer days under the canopy, the songs of generations of birds, and I understood beauty, then, better than I could ever hope to convey in words or ever again to myself in my quiet moments alone. I went to the tree, wending my way through the field as a vole or a garter snake might, and sat under its shelter, and there, I slept.

When I woke up, the crickets still sang, but a dim morning mist had crawled across us, chilling my hands and feet numb. I had brought my camera, thank goodness, but the rest of my things remained over at the segment of barn wall, probably soaked through with dew.

"You wanted to see what lay beneath my skin," said a willowy voice at my right hand. Laurel Bolton's cool, silk-smooth hand folded over mine. She lay in the same position she had been in before her transformation, head back against the trunk as though she were too tired to hold it up fully.

"Why did you trust me?" I asked.

"Because I think you have the potential to tell the truth. It is too late for the truth to heal me, but you can help others. And you will."

I wanted to say that I didn't have the luxury of telling the truth. I wanted to explain the game, and the skewed rules everyone played by, and my own feeling that my truth wasn't worth anything. After all, where had truth gotten this woman, this dryad, whatever she was? She was going to die, despite her still, small voice of truth, because she simply could not tell enough.

After sitting in silence a moment, she spoke again.

"Perhaps you would like to ask me your questions again. Things always fit together better after a good sleep."

I turned on my camera, knelt beside her, and began again.

"Why have you decided to come and protest the mall again, with rumours circulating that your health is in decline?"

"This is my home. I have to defend it the best I know how."

"What made you decide to fight for this particular cause?"

"The Trees are my family. We all share the earth, and I am part of the balance of life here."

"Why don't you take more dramatic steps to get out into the world and make yourself known?"

"I have a daughter. I would never do anything to put her in danger."

This time, when I finished, I had to wipe away the streams of tears coursing down my face.

I know my editors may reject this part of my life story, and I do know why. However, as I grow older, I've found myself growing sad in my quiet moments, that the greatest truth of my life is one which I can never truly share with anybody. But nevertheless, Laurel Bolton, and her beautiful tree, taught me that real stories do not run in a straight line, beginning, middle, end. They are a spiral, like the rings inside of an old tree, layer upon layer of meaning seeping across borders, alternate paths lurking just beyond the edges of the story that is told. Writers, truth tellers of all sorts, walk the maze, follow the spiral, and the best ones manage to get close to the center, after years of crawling through on their knees.

For one, shining moment, I saw the center of Laurel Bolton's being, and I will remember that glimpse until the end of my days.

About The Authors

Jennifer Bickley

A recent English and Writing graduate, retail salesperson and aspiring writer, Jennifer Bickley has writen for years, but has only recently evolved from fan fiction to original science fiction and fantasy. With the love and encouragement of her fiance (and two cats), she plans on continuing that evolution. In addition to her writing, Jennifer also runs her own editing business, 'The Queen's English', editing technical and business documents, as well as fiction. Email her at jennbickley@hotmail.com for details.

Elizabeth Hirst

Elizabeth Hirst is an author, animator and indie publisher from Oakville, Ontario. She has a Master's Degree in English Literature, attended the Odyssey Workshop, Class of 2006 as one of the youngest attendees up until that point, and graduated from Sheridan College's Bachelor of Arts Animation Program with a specialization in 3D work. She has lived all of her life in Southern Ontario, and her experiences there inform the structure and feel of almost all of her work. Her contact information, and website, can be found on the first page of this book.

Ira Nayman

Writer. Performer. Famous racquetball couch. Ira Nayman has written five books of science fiction journalism in the Alternate Reality News Service series, and one novel, Welcome to the Multiverse (Sorry for the Inconvenience). His second novel, You Can't Kill the Multiverse (But You Can Mess With its Head) is scheduled for publication by Britain's Elsewhen Press in January, 2014. In 2010, he won the Swift Satire Writing Contest. Les Pages aux Folles, Ira's Web site of political satire and surreal cartoons (updated weekly), had its 11th birthday on September 1, 2013. But, seriously, it's nothing you couldn't do…if you just put your mind to it…

Tecuma Macintyre

A transplanted native of the 'wild crazy that is Florida', Tecuma shares space with four hundred books (at current count!) and three tyrannical felines. This is her first published short story, and when she's not working at Barnes and Noble, or with her nose stuck in a book, she can be found traipsing across the wilds of Azeroth in World of Warcraft. Her email is dame.macintyre@gmail.com

And, for exclusive content, updates and fun, connect with us online at:

Twitter: @PopSeagullPub
Website/Blog: http://popseagullpublishing.wordpress.com/
Smashwords: http://www.smashwords.com/profile/view/pop-seagullpublishing

Thank you for reading with
Pop Seagull Publishing!

If you enjoyed this book, then why not try

Monsters and Mist

A collection of fantasy short stories by
Elizabeth Hirst

Do battle with a carnivorous alien disguised as a garden!

Follow a young boy as he discovers the sinister truth behind the Teddy Bears' Picnic!

Journey with a young woman into a far away land where the sky is an ocean, and it's sprung a leak!

All this, and more awaits you in this compact anthology, available in print from Createspace, in e-book from Smashwords, and in person at a fan event near you!

Please enjoy this preview of:

Distant Early Warning

Pop Seagull's next novel by Elizabeth Hirst for Spring 2014

After global warming, Felicia Dennigan lives in a world of constant rainstorms, poverty and struggle. She considers herself safe from the stories of 'Screamers', dead people rising from the grave up north and driving people mad with their cries, until one night, she sees a news reel of her father, dead and screaming. In order to solve her father's murder, Denny must navigate a Northern Ontario transformed into a playground for hungry ghosts, with nothing but a backpack and her loyal dog for company.

Chapter One
The Squatters from Up North

Felicia Dennigan, 'Denny' to her friends, pulled her book bag onto her lap so that a man in a well-worn plaid shirt could squeeze in beside her. She breathed in, tentatively, through her nose. This one smelled of fry grease. There were much worse smells on the bus—just this morning, for example, she'd smelled some. She normally avoided sitting beside people who made a fuss, or smelled like pee, or made inappropriate conversation because their wife had just left them, by leaving her bag on the seat next to her, but the bus was nearing the station, and it had become far too crowded for people to keep a polite distance from one another.

Felicia had a book in her bag, several in fact, but she left them there. She had been reading and analyzing books all day. Mentally, it was time to mellow out in front of the TV, but she had to get home for that. Denny leaned against the bus's damp window frame and watched the bright signs of downtown St. Catharines drag by. She also wondered how the bus driver could see out of the side windows when they were covered with an inch of road grime. There was the Oasis, with its bright red-and-yellow, and a couple of new nightclubs that Denny wondered if anybody really went to. Downtown St. Catharines had a lot of nightclubs that flitted in and out of existence in the blink of an eye, tacky places in badly-wired old buildings along the St. Paul strip. A lot of them were flop houses now, but some of them still kept going, changing hands every few months. There was something transient about them, like the people themselves, the ones that came down from the North looking for jobs, shelter, anything they could lay their hands on with their homes and their livings gone.

The bus turned into the bus station, then came to a stop accompanied by the squeal of the brakes and the acrid smell of burning rubber. Denny picked up her book bag and squeezed it to her chest, keeping one hand on the zipper pulls and the other on the pockets. She thanked the bus driver, stepped down the stairs, and entered the odiferous crowd of beggars, pedlars and thieves surrounding the bus.

Some people at school put padlocks on their bags, but Denny lived cheap, and she liked that the bag hugged to her chest doubled as a sort of 'bag-ering ram' to separate the crowd in front of her without her having to shove. She didn't really like to shove people out of her way, as she suspected some of the others in her class did. Class…a funny word, that…especially when only a lucky few could afford school.

Hands appeared in front of Denny's face—dirty hands, attached to tired-looking people in tired-looking clothes. There were native people, and Asians, but most of them were white, and all of them had faces full of creases, as if fear and hunger, those great feral tigers, had dragged unyielding claws down their faces.

"Money, please," cried a woman with rotting teeth, "A quarter, anything!"

Denny shook her head, and the beggar retracted her hands. She had stopped carrying cash a long time ago, less because of pickpockets, and more because her empathy had been costing her upwards of twenty dollars a week.

A skinny teen in ripped jeans and a t-shirt pulled from the charity bin at one of the downtown churches bumped into her shoulder. It changed Denny's angle slightly, and as she turned, someone at the edge of the crowd caught her eye. She popped a wide grin, instantly, without realizing that she was showing her crooked front teeth. It couldn't be…but he was due for a visit. Long overdue, in fact, but Denny had had a feeling, from the moment she got up that morning, that she would hear from him. Her father's visits were irregular, and far fewer between even than his calls or postcards, but when she got that feeling in her gut, that deep-down excitement, the phone would always ring, or, if fortune smiled down on her that day, she would hear a knock on the door.

After Dad's last visit, just after Christmas (he had apologized for missing the big day, although most years he did, and brought her a tattered copy of Blake's Songs of Innocence and

Experience he had dug up in a used book store in Waterloo) the feeling in Denny's gut had receded and not come back until today. Today was June 30, 2050. Even for somebody like Dad, with no permanent address, six months was a long time-- too long for Denny.

    That man, standing on the edge of the crowd...Denny forgot her normal scruples and shoved people out of the way. Short, heavy-set, with dark brown hair like hers and a brown bomber jacket, the man had to be him. Denny shifted her bag to one hand and put the other out like a quarterback, eager to get to him.

    The man in the bomber jacket turned around, and his face was jowly, covered with stubble. His ears stuck out, and so did his nose. In fact, he didn't even have the right skin tone to be Dad...he was definitely Middle-Eastern. Dad was Irish.

    Denny stopped cold, as the crowd dispersed around her, the beggars and thieves moving out to catch the number seventeen and the number two buses, which were pulling up to Platform A. The man in the bomber jacket shot her a dirty look, and Denny realized with some embarrassment that she had been staring at him. She scurried into the glassed-in waiting area, swiping her pass over the scanner at the door to prove she was a paying customer.

    Inside, the waiting area smelled like cooking pizza and tracked-in mud. With no admittance for vagabonds, the rows of metal mesh benches were almost empty, except for a few old ladies in plastic rain bonnets and young people in fast food uniforms slouched against the windows. It had been almost six straight days of muggy heat in the mornings, breaking into torrential rain in the afternoon and continuing on all night until the cycle began again. Even with the air conditioning on in the waiting area, the Great Lakes humidity hung in the air, making breathing a bit like drinking an insubstantial soup.

    Denny felt her heart thumping in her chest as she sat down on one of the many empty benches. Why did she always have to see his face in crowds? Why did so many characters on TV remind her of him? It happened too often...too often for a grown woman. Grown women accepted the exigencies of life, and moved on. She sighed and placed her head in her hands.

Her wavy, thick auburn hair spilled into her field of vision, waving gently to and fro, taunting her. People had always known she was Sean Dennigan's girl because of that unruly crop of hair. Wild and curly it had been, until she straightened it. She could walk into a shop two hours behind Dad, and if she got the same cashier, she would get picked out as a relative. Denny had found it funny, at the time, but when she looked back, she just longed to belong like that again, to have someone with whom she could be identified. For those brief times when Dad decided to stay in St. Catharines, for a night, or a week, or during good times, without any episodes, two weeks, Denny could introduce him to her friends. She could take him out to restaurants and not ask for separate bills. He would talk to her, and not try to discuss the intricacies of literature as spouted by Professor So-and-So or how much he knew about everything (an irritating trait of University men, especially at parties). They could remember things together...things that meant something, like losing her first tooth, or the time that Mom got caught in the sprinklers at Cave Springs golf course.

The ding of a bell cut into Denny's thoughts. She raised her head out of her hands.

Bus Number Eighteen is now arriving at Platform F.

--Said the rolling LED sign above the waiting area.

Denny picked up her things and headed for the door. Grown women did not wallow in misery in deserted bus stations. Grown women got themselves home, to a glass of lemonade and the evening news, and attempted to forget the things they could not change.

. . .

Denny left the bus at the corner of Welland and George Street, and began the short walk home. The neighborhood was filled with old Victorians and the new housing that had sprung up from their graves, brick structures, mostly, with sagging porches and more character than insulation. Denny loved the old-growth trees along the walkways, and the unruly character of most of the lawns.

She reached the end of the walkway leading up to the house she shared with three other students, lucky number one-thirteen, a small brick house with yellowed siding and a screened-in porch. Like most of the houses on the street, it boasted a big, gnarled maple with cracks in its bark as deep as fault lines. The poor old thing had seen thousands of better days, Denny thought as her shoes crackled over the gravel drive. Like all old trees these days, black patches of rot crawled over its trunk, a nasty side-effect of all the extra rain that had swept over the peninsula lately.

Some kids in ill-fitting overalls, Northern squatters' kids from down the street, swarmed across the lawn, brandishing fallen sticks from last night's rainstorm. One of the boys was wearing the frames to a pair of thick black glasses, taped along one arm. The neighborhood kids had been wired for a week after old Mrs. Jones gave them those—now their Harry Potter games could acquire an extra layer of realism.

Little Harry Potter whacked the old maple on the lawn with an especially big stick. The others followed suit.

"Take that, Voldemort! Expecto Patronum!" said Potter.

"Exthpelliarmuth!" said a little blonde girl with a gap between her teeth.

Denny climbed up the sloping lawn to the tree, and laid a hand on it. The kids stopped, and stared at her. She had become somewhat of a neighborhood guru after giving Jason Mandrake, the boy whose family squatted in her backyard, an old copy of the Harry Potter series, which was subsequently passed around to every child on the street.

"Hey, guys, this isn't Voldemort...it's just an old tree...he... be-spelled," she said, hoping to distract them from knocking off any more bark that the tree couldn't spare, "But you know where I did see him? Down by the fire hydrant on the corner."

Little Potter's eyes widened, solemn and deadly serious.

"Let's get him!" he called to the others, and soon enough the kids had flocked away off of number one-thirteen's lawn, toward the fire hydrant on the corner.

Denny patted the tree like the shoulder of an old friend during a shared joke. She wasn't so sure she and the tree hadn't shared a joke, anyway.

The presence of the children had reminded Denny that it was rent collection day. The girls took turns collecting money from the squatters in the backyard, and this month, it was Denny's turn. She made her way down the empty driveway, to the grey garden gate, and knocked. The latch was easy to pick from the other side, but Denny never intruded on the Mandrake's scant privacy.

At the back of the house, she could smell multiple aromas that, because of the damp, stagnant air, had not been apparent at the front. The first was smoke, and meat, corresponding with the plume of campfire smoke rising over the privacy fence. The second was laundry soap (Denny wondered where squatters had got real laundry soap, but she applauded the feat), and the third, much less pleasant to the nose, was baby diaper, sour and somehow powdery.

Mrs. Mandrake answered the garden door. She was a thin woman, once genteel, with brassy blonde hair and sharp lines around her mouth. She wore a patched, stained button-down shirt that was probably a nice pink stripe once, and a picked brown flare skirt. In one arm, she carried a girl baby, and in the other, a knife.

Her dour expression softened when she recognized Denny.

"Oh, Denny, it's you," she said, "I thought it was Yasmeen again to complain about the noise."

Denny stepped into the yard—the Mandrakes' home, for what it was worth. There, a long stretch of tarp (several tarps, actually, duct-taped together) covered their living space, a complex of crate pieces nailed together and supported in places with broomsticks. Underneath, plastic Rubbermaid crates doubled as storage space for all their worldly possessions, and a means of keeping their sleeping bags off the ground. Jason, their seven-year old, poked at a glowing fire with a stick. A miserable place to live—but every available room in the house was full, including the living room couch, and most houses nowadays were the same. Hopefully, the government would finish the relief camps soon, so people like the Mandrakes could at least have a state-issued tent to live in.

Mrs. Mandrake had been a secretary, or so she said, for a lumber concern in Thunder Bay. Mr. Mandrake had run a

landscaping business. Both of them had lost everything when the Screamers rose. The dead had risen from the ground, at night, and chased families from their homes, and screamed, and screamed, in a strange gibberish language that pierced the ears and warped the senses. People had gone mad in those first three months, unable to sleep, and unable to rationalize what was happening to them.
No one in Ontario had believed the refugees at first, because who, in the age of cell phones and the internet and all of the other trappings of modern-day life, would believe that the dead could actually rise? And yet, the North was rapidly emptying itself...and there were the testimonies, thousands upon thousands of them...

Denny had believed the Mandrakes, even before True North Media Corp. had gone up North and gotten the first national broadcast out. As someone who read made-up stories all day, Denny could recognize a yarn, and Mrs. Mandrake told stories that no one could or would make up.

For instance, there was Mr. Mandrake's old business partner, the stone wholesaler, who jumped into a river glen after one of the Screamers turned out to be his brother. That one always gave Denny the chills. Ghosts, wraiths, zombies... that was one outlandish thing, but having one as part of the family? You'd never escape them, or the memory of what they had become, for as long as you lived.

And Dad was still missing.

Denny shook off her macabre thoughts. People like the Mandrakes didn't need any more negativity flowing their way.

"It's that time again, Mrs. M. It's my turn to collect the rent."

Denny cringed for Mrs. Mandrake's inevitable arguments, the reasons (all true) that she didn't have this month's rent: The rising price of fresh food. Little Jay Jay growing out of his jeans. Needing to go across town to the doctor on the bus. Denny prepared to argue, and prepared to feel bad for the rest of the night.
As much as the Mandrakes didn't have money, neither did she. She had covered for them before, to keep them away from the wrath of Yasmeen, but the money had come out of her savings. She'd had to borrow textbooks from a classmate one semester in order to make up the money—and that had been a close call for her grades. No

grades, no education. No education, no ticket inland, away from the flooding.

Mrs. Mandrake set her knife down on a bloody piece of newspaper, where she had been cubing some beef. She wiped her hands off on her apron.

"I've got your money, for once. There's something else we need to take care of first, though."

Jason left the fire. He had a lean, freckled face, and wore jeans ripped at the knee.

"I want to keep him! Let me keep him!" he said, dancing around his mother. Mrs. Mandrake stilled him with a firm hand on his shoulder.

"We've got no money, Jay Jay. The only way he stays is if he eats your meals."

"Keep who?" Denny asked. The feeling in her stomach spread out, grew sour.

Mrs. Mandrake did not answer. She led Denny along the board fence, painted an ugly, peeling brown. Jason trailed behind them, sulking. They crossed the yard, to where another alleyway extended down the house between the wall and a chain-link fence. This gap dead-ended at the front of the house, and was barely wide enough for a person to squeeze down sideways. For as long as Denny had lived at the house, they had kept old clay pots and faded-out plastic lawn ornaments back there. Denny wasn't sure what they were storing them for—they probably came from previous owners, back in the time when only one family lived here.

A section of white plastic garden trellis tipped upward, then fell over. From underneath it crawled a black and white Border Collie, his shaggy fur tipped with mud. He held his tail down, and kept his ears pulled back. Ratty blue collar. Bone-shaped license tags.

Denny's stomach flipped over into full-scale nausea then.

"Geoff," she said, kneeling down and putting her arms out, "Come here, boy. It's okay."

Geoff wagged his tail, although he remained low to the ground. He crept toward Denny and flopped over onto her feet, the tip of his tail still wagging and his eyes as large and glassy as shooting marbles. Denny scratched his head, ignoring the gross, dander-y substance that collected on her fingers when she did so. Geoff stretched up toward her face, and licked her chin.

"This is my Dad's dog. Geoff shouldn't be here without Dad," she said.

"Someone kicked him out of a car onto our front lawn this morning, and we let him into the backyard. Ever since, he's been cowering in that pile of junk."

"You never saw a man with him? A man with curly hair, and an old bomber jacket?" Denny said, standing up. Geoff migrated over to her right hand, placing his head directly underneath it as a not-so-subtle-hint. Denny petted him absently, lost in a sea of half-formed, fearful thoughts.

Mrs. Mandrake shook her head. "Denny, I've seen your Father before. He wasn't here. I'm sorry."

"Right..." Denny said, heading for the steps to the back porch, and the square of cool darkness visible through the screen door. Geoff followed her, not leaving her magical right hand for a moment. Denny wondered how long it had been since someone had petted him.

"Denny!" called Mrs. Mandrake, as she squeezed the handle to open the screen door.

"What?"

"I've still got rent for you."

Denny pulled the screen door open. She let Geoff slip inside before her. "Could you put it in the mail slot? I have to make a few calls."

She would also have to find a place to hide the dog.

Made in the USA
Charleston, SC
19 September 2013